Sinfully SCARRED

RECKLESS BASTARDS MC
MAYHEM

WALL STREET JOURNAL & USA TODAY BESTSELLING AUTHOR
KB WINTERS

Copyright and Disclaimer

This book is a work of fiction. The names, characters, places and incidents are products of the writer's imagination and have been used fictitiously and are not to be construed as real. Any resemblance to persons, living or dead, actual events, locales or organizations is entirely coincidental.

Copyright © 2018 Book Boyfriends Publishing

All rights reserved. No part of this publication may be reproduced, stored in or introduced into a retrieval system, or transmitted, in any form, or by any means (electronic, mechanical, photocopying, recording, or otherwise) without the prior written permission of the copyright owner. The author acknowledges the trademarked status and trademark owners of various products referenced in this work of fiction, which have been used without permission. The publication/use of the trademarks is not authorized, associated with, or sponsored by the trademark owners.

Table of Contents

Copyright and Disclaimer ii

Chapter 1 7

Chapter 2 15

Chapter 3 33

Chapter 4 39

Chapter 5 57

Chapter 6 73

Chapter 7 85

Chapter 8 103

Chapter 9 121

Chapter 10 143

Chapter 11... 171

Chapter 12 187

Chapter 13 199

Chapter 14 211

Chapter 15 223

Chapter 16 237

Chapter 17 251

Chapter 18 263

Chapter 19 271

Chapter 20 279

Chapter 21 293

Chapter 22 299

Chapter 23 313

Chapter 24 331

Sinfully Scarred

Reckless Bastards MC

By Wall Street Journal & USA Today Bestselling Author

KB Winters

Chapter 1

Tate

"Whoo boy, you sure you can handle all this power?" Cross, the President of the Reckless Bastards MC shouted at me over the quick-fire shots of a semi-automatic.

I grinned at his wide smile. Cross was a big ass kid at heart, but he took his club responsibilities seriously, which was why he'd come over when I said I'd be at the clubhouse today. "I can more than handle it," I told him and flexed my biceps.

"Good to hear, because those young honeys over there are checkin' out the goods." He wiggled his eyebrows as three half-dressed women made their way over to us.

I turned just in time to clock them. Two brunettes and a blonde, all hot and leggy with fake tits as big as hot air balloons. The blonde was the apparent leader of the threesome, pushing her tits out as she approached. "Hey boys, we were wondering if you did private lessons?"

Cross smiled and clapped me on the back. "No, but I'm sure we could make an exception for a group of pretty ladies. Isn't that right, Golden Boy?"

I flashed what I hoped was a polite smile but the truth was these women did nothing to make my cock stir, which was damned annoying. Before being locked up, I would've taken all three to a dark corner and made sure they all left with smiles on their faces. Now, I felt jack shit. "Cross here is the boss and the best person to teach you to shoot."

The blonde's smile dimmed at my obvious brush off. "And maybe you could give us some after-hours lessons?"

"Sorry, busy." I turned to Max who silently watched everything with a surprised look on his face.

"Whatever," she said with a pout and I was sure if I gave enough of a damn to turn around, those collagen-enhanced lips would be poking out like a fucking kid. "We need more ammo. Cross, was it?"

"Sure thing, sugar. Follow me."

"That was...unexpected."

I looked up at my older brother who constantly looked worried about me, which I appreciated as much as I fucking hated it. "I'm not interested, all right?"

Max held up his hands, a smirk on his face. "It's fine by me. I've got a great woman at home to love up on anytime I want."

I smiled because I couldn't have chosen a better woman for my brother. Jana was sweet and beautiful and had gone through a hell similar to his. They understood each other and to me, that shit was special. "And when I feel like having one, I will too."

"I know you will. How are things are going at the shop?"

I nodded, talking as we both began to break down and clean the returned guns. "Everything is set, mostly. I hope to have the grand opening by the end of the week." I used a small portion of the money I'd gotten in my lawsuit to open up a tattoo shop. At least I'd gotten something from the assholes who locked me up for six years for a fucking crime I didn't commit. As a kid, I'd had dreams of being an artist but coming from a poor single parent home, I couldn't afford such lofty dreams and enlisted in the Army. But this money, this fucking blood money, had given me a chance to make a future I'd always wanted.

"I know it doesn't change anything, but that money is freedom bro."

I nodded because I knew that. Still, the three million I got—a half million for each year inside—plus the fifteen in punitive damages after it had come out that the cops and prosecutor had hidden exculpatory evidence, felt like hush money. Like I wasn't supposed to be angry about the years stolen from me. Well I was angry, dammit. "Doesn't mean this shit doesn't suck, Max."

"No doubt, but that anger might get you locked up again. Legit this time, though."

That was my biggest fear, that after the shit show my life had been for six years and three and a half months, I'd end up right back in that hellhole. "I'm working on it." I wasn't really but staying away from the club for the past few months had helped. Not that I blamed them for what had happened, I didn't. But I felt out of sorts, uneasy around the people who were my family.

If not for Max and Jana, I probably would've already lost my shit a few times over. Cross returned with a smile on his face, and a telltale pink lipstick spot on his neck. "Love blondes...so fucking much," he said with a groan.

Max snorted. "Natural?"

He shrugged. "Who gives a fuck?" He laughed and stared at the women, holding guns all wrong, but having a blast anyway. "A minute," he said to me, his expression now business-like.

"What's up," I asked back inside the office of the RB Gun Range.

"Do you still want to be a Reckless Bastard, Golden Boy?"

I frowned. "What the fuck kind of question is that? I'm here ain't I?" What the fuck else did they want from me?

"It seems like you don't want shit to do with us, and I'm not the only one feeling that way," he bit out angrily. I understood his anger. It was his job as president to make sure we could rely on our fellow brothers when we needed them.

"Shit yeah, I do, Cross. Put yourself in my position, six years lost and not a goddamn thing you can do about it. Having people treat you like a fucking sideshow everywhere you go. Even the clubhouse. I came back to you guys because you're my family. My friends. But if you think that camaraderie and shit makes up for what I lost, it sure as fuck doesn't. And hearing the guys act like I somehow *came up*, pisses me the fuck off."

I shook my head and kicked the ugly green metal desk that Cross must have picked up at a garage sale in the seventies. "I'm putting in my time here at the range, providing security for the dispensary and I've got two brothers set up to work for me at the shop. What the fuck else do you want?"

Cross stared at me; his dark blue eyes missed nothing. He wasn't happy, but he understood. "I want you to get laid so you're not such a miserable fucking bastard, but hey, you do you."

"You go rot in prison for another man's crime and then tell me how you feel, Prez. Later." I stood and yanked the door open, storming out of the range with an angry wave to Max. Like I needed this shit.

I crossed the large blacktop parking lot that separated the gun range from the clubhouse, hopped on my bike and took my ass home. Where I could be alone.

Chapter 2

Teddy

Not many jobs would allow me the time for a late morning swim, but it was one of the perks of working for myself. This week included lots of downtime, well not exactly downtime so much as planning for an upcoming consultation with yet another reality TV couple. Not that I had anything against reality stars, but they were newly rich without the accompanying taste. But I gave them what they wanted, a lavish wedding befitting their new status as D-list celebrities.

Ugh. Now wasn't the time to think about them—this time was mine. After a good thirty minutes of laps back and forth across the pool, I turned over on my back and let my body float. I got to relax in a way I didn't always get to do, especially in public. People always stared at me and I wasn't being full of myself, it was just the truth. They either recognized me as the former runway model and cover girl and wanted to know what I'd been up to. They loved to tell me how much of a shame it was that I'd lost everything, because to them, losing the fame and the money *was* everything. The others? They just told me how fucked up it was that my limp marred the runway I'd spent my youth perfecting.

I went out and I used my sharp tongue to weed out the jerks and rubberneckers, and I usually had my best friend Jana at my side. Reluctantly, but still, at my side. Days like today, I preferred privacy and used the pool at the rehab center where I still did the occasional round of physical therapy to keep my muscles loose and strong. The old people usually gave me a smile and a wave, sometimes the occasional wink and the few kids were so focused on their own therapy, they paid me no attention.

"Hey lady."

Must've spoken too soon. I looked over and spotted a black-haired kid with the lightest blue eyes I'd ever seen. "What's up, kiddo?" He couldn't be more than seven or eight, two lanes away from me with a bright grin on his face.

"What happened to your leg?"

I stifled the groan that wanted to escape at his question—hell, it was everyone's question. I liked kids, when they were quiet, but most of them were too damn curious. Still, I couldn't bring myself to be mean to the adorable little twerp. "I was in a car accident that broke my leg in several places."

To his credit the kid didn't ask to get an up close and personal look at the zipper scar that ran the length of my left leg. "I have a scar too, see?" He lifted his shirt to reveal what was clearly some type of heart surgery. "But when I get older I'm gonna get a Superman tattooed right here," he smacked the spot with a proud grin. "My mom says it's a sign that I made it, just like Superman, nothing can kill him."

"Hey, you're pretty smart for a kid."

"Thanks. You're a pretty cool for a grownup." He waved and turned onto his back as he began to float away. "You're a girl, maybe flowers or something for your leg!"

I shook my head. Even when they were young, men couldn't help giving out unwanted advice. "Yeah, thanks kid."

I couldn't help but think about his words though, even days later as I prepared for my meeting with Ron Hardy and Tessa McMann, the winners of the most recent season of *I Wanna Fall In Love*. They'd postponed their consultation until her latest boob job had a chance to heal, which meant I was free to attend the grand opening of GET INK'D, the tattoo shop owned by Max's younger brother Tate.

I didn't really relish hanging around with a bunch of bikers all night, but Max was good people and completely in love with Jana, and until he proved otherwise—that meant Tate was good too. The only problem I had with him was he was too much man. Too big, too much hair and a smile that could drop even the tightest pair of panties. "Congratulations, Tate. The place looks good."

He flashed that damn smile and leaned in. "Thank you, Teddy. You're looking pretty damn good yourself."

I rolled my eyes at his over the top flirting, but I never took him seriously. It was just a little innocent flirting and I knew it was harmless because he hadn't made a move in all the months I'd known him. It was nice though, being able to flirt without any inappropriate blowback. Besides, my sharp tongue didn't seem to faze Tate. If anything, he seemed amused by it. "Thanks. I did it just for you."

He shook his head, his hair falling around his shoulders. "Not possible. If you'd dressed for me, you'd be wearing a lot less."

I looked at him seriously before a laugh escaped. "I'll keep that in mind for your next grand opening." The place was nice even though it was set up like pretty much every tattoo shop ever. The artwork however, was incredible. "Did you draw this stuff?"

"Yeah, you like it?"

I nodded as I looked around, spotting Jana looking uncomfortable as hell, surrounded by Max's biker brothers. "You're very talented, Tate. Can we set up a consultation?"

His golden brows rose in surprise. "Sure, but you don't strike me as the tattoo type."

I grinned, but I rolled my eyes just so he knew how ridiculous he sounded. "Yeah, well there's a lot you don't know about me, *Golden Boy*."

Amusement flashed in his gray eyes that could, under the right circumstances, really get my motor going. But he was too close to my life to go there. With his hand to his chest, Tate feigned hurt. "You don't think I look like a Golden Boy?"

I couldn't help but smile at his playfulness. I'd been through some shit in my life, but if I'd gone through what Tate had, wrongfully imprisoned for six years, I would be pissed off all the damn time. "You do have kind of a whole *golden thing* going on," I told him and took him in. Without the tattoos, long hair and big muscles, he could have easily been like the suits who thought they deserved a woman like me. "But you do have really great hair."

He snorted and rolled his eyes. "Yeah, thanks. Just what every guy wants to hear."

"Oh, come on, Golden Boy, I'm sure your ego can handle it. Besides you seem to have a whole fan club over there." I nodded in the direction of a group of rough looking women blatantly staring at us.

"They're like that with everyone," he grunted with disgust.

Against my better judgment, I dropped a hand on his shoulder. "Poor baby, not feeling too special on his big night?"

Instead of throwing a tantrum, he waggled his eyebrows. "I *am* special, sweetheart."

All I could do was roll my eyes at him. "Do we need to set up an appointment or anything? I've never had a tattoo consultation before." That kids' words had really stuck with me. I wasn't the wilting flower type so there was no reason for me to play the part.

"Sure, lets." He grinned with a sparkle in his eyes. "Since I'm a businessman and all. How about I come up with a few drawings and you think up some ideas?"

"Thank you, Tate." I couldn't even describe how grateful I was that I could talk to him without worrying about…anything, really. I handed him my phone. "Put your information in and I'll try not to stalk you."

He flashed another boyish grin. "I make no promises," he said and handed the phone back to me.

"Right. See you soon, *Golden Boy*." I left the man of the hour and headed for my girl Jana and her fiancé. "Hey guys, how's it going?"

Jana shrugged, a sure sign she was feeling all kinds of uncomfortable. "It's going."

Max wrapped an arm around her waist and tucked her under his arm. "Whenever you're ready, say the word babe." He dropped a kiss on her forehead and Jana looked down, using her hair to cover the scar on her face.

"No way, tonight is Tate's big night. He needs our support."

"Jana, do his books if you want to support him. Don't stay and be uncomfortable, unless of course I'm asking you to." Just as I hoped, she smiled and rolled her eyes.

Max flashed a grin filled with gratitude. "That's a good idea. Go tell him and I'll take you home."

"Don't worry Max, I'll take her. I need some time with my girl anyway."

"Thanks, Teddy."

"Don't mention it, Max." I stood by the door, ignoring the angry stares of the women who looked like they were rode hard and put away wet and the looks of the bikers, probably imagining me naked.

If only they knew, I thought to myself with a grin.

***

"He actually said he couldn't believe I was still so hot," I griped on the phone to Jana as I drove home from the office. "And then he told me I could make big money on reality TV. I wanted to choke that motherfucker, Jana."

I heard her snicker down the line and it made me smile. "Those reality people think no one has ever made the money they make, Teddy. It's good no one knows how rich you are."

"You're right, but it still pisses me off." I was half tempted to rub strawberries all over his face, but anaphylaxis was a surefire way to end my business. "Anyway, how are you?"

She sighed and I swear I could hear her smile. "Good. Work has been great, but busy. Max wants to get married sooner rather than later."

"Of course he does, the man is cuckoo for you. You still want to marry him, right?"

"Hell yeah I do! I love Max, it's just hard to believe this is happening."

"Not if you know you—which I do. Trust me, this is exactly what's supposed to happen for you."

She sighed heavily, still not accustomed to accepting compliments. "Thanks, Teddy. I called to invite you to dinner tonight."

"Sure," I told her absently as I walked up the five steps to my little split-level home. Blue roses in a beautiful crystal vase were on my stoop. No card or note, and a gold box that looked like it held lingerie or chocolate. "Did you send me flowers?"

"No, maybe it was one of your clients?"

"Unlikely," I scoffed. "They'd never get something so subdued, trust me." I got a weird feeling about the flowers, because no delivery person would simply leave them out like this.

I chose to leave the items on the porch, went inside and kicked off my shoes. The truth was, the reason I went so hardcore on physical therapy and fitness was due to my love of expensive shoes — not because I was an image conscious former model. "What's for dinner?"

"Why don't you show up and find out?"

I laughed. "Oooh, my little kitten has claws. Rawr!"

She laughed. "Come whenever, crazy lady. Bye."

Jana was the best friend I'd ever had. The only real friend I'd ever had who didn't want something from me, other than my friendship. I loved her for that, but I also loved her delicious home cooking. I showered and changed, ignoring the packages on my porch as I exited the house again and made my way to Jana's place.

When I arrived, I noticed a bike in the driveway, but that wasn't all that uncommon since Max pretty much lived there these days.

Before Jana met Max, I'd walk right in. Now, I knocked. Every damn time. Walking in on my best friend getting rammed by the love of her life wasn't something I ever wanted to see. Not again.

The door opened to reveal a smiling blond, but not the one I was expecting. "Here for the free food too?"

"And the company. How's the tattoo business, Tate?"

He shrugged and stood back to let me in. "So far, so good. Need to do some marketing shit to keep up the steady flow but you know how it is."

"I do. If you need tips, ask." Jana stood at the counter tossing a salad with a satisfied grin of a woman who'd recently had an orgasm. "Damn J, you look hot!"

She looked up with a blush. "Thanks Teddy but it's just a dress."

"Tell that to Marilyn's iconic white dress." Her blush deepened and I gave her break. "So this is like a full on party, huh?"

"Not at all, but I felt like cooking and figured I'd invite our two favorite people. You okay?"

I sighed and put on my best catalog model smile. "Sure, just a bit tired. Brides are the worst!" I laughed and wrapped her up in a hug, feeling uncharacteristically touchy-feely today. "You need some help?"

"You remember how to make that vinaigrette I showed you?"

"Do I? I only make it once a day, so I think I got this." Back when it became clear that my modeling career was over, the first thing I learned how to do was cook to avoid eating out every night. Okay, to avoid *going out* every night. But meeting Jana had taught me that I didn't know what cooking was until she showed me her skills. She smiled as I began to move around her kitchen, pulling out ingredients. "Where's Max?"

"The grill," she said with a soft smile. "He loves my cooking but he says, she lowered her voice in a mock Max voice, "'grilling is man's work.'"

That was such a Max thing to say. The man wasn't a chauvinist or a pig, but he had a mile-wide protective streak and I appreciated that about him. "Just be sure he thinks cleaning that bad boy is *also* men's work."

She laughed and picked up the mac & cheese that made my stomach stand up and protest its hunger. "I'll let you tell him that."

"Why me? You're the one he sees naked, use that to your advantage."

"Let's go, cuckoo bird. We're eating in the backyard tonight."

We ate out in the yard a lot, especially now that Jana had decked it all out, making it the perfect place to entertain almost year-round thanks to the mostly mild weather in Mayhem. I thought about the flowers on my stoop. It still gave me a strange feeling, but I couldn't even describe it if I'd wanted to. And with two overprotective former service members, I really had no desire to bring up my suspicions now.

Besides who in the hell would stalk me? I was a party planner. A damn good one, but still, not exactly living a high-risk lifestyle.

"Hey, you okay?" Tate looked at me halfway through dinner, his gray eyes shining with concern.

I slapped a smile on my face, which he clearly didn't buy, and nodded. "Yep, I'm good. Thanks. How are you?"

His lips twitched with amusement. "Getting better every day."

"Glad to hear it," I said and tapped my glass to his beer bottle. "To getting better."

He grinned and tapped my glass again.

By the time the meal was over and the dishes were done, I felt better but still uneasy. That gift had me rattled and I'd learned in the early days of my modeling career to listen to my gut. It was how I avoided being left alone with certain photographers and models, and why I had a reputation as a good girl, because I didn't go to parties where kids had no business being. Right now, I was getting those same vibes.

"Hey, are you sure you're all right," Jana asked.

"Just a little frazzled. I'll be fine after a good night of rest."

"Okay. If you're sure," she said but she didn't believe me. "I'll let that answer slide. Tonight. Tomorrow, we're talking about it."

"Damn, look who's gotten bossy as hell."

"Between you and Max, I had to adapt." The pink on her face and neck told the whole story. Jana was still getting used to voicing her opinions. "Tomorrow," she said and pointed a finger my way.

"Tomorrow," I agreed as I stepped out into the slightly cooler, but still warm, night air.

"Hey, you want me to follow you home? You seem spooked."

Dammit, was Tate a decent guy too? "Thanks for the offer, but I'm fine. I swear."

"Be safe," he said as he hopped on his bike, started it and drove off like a rocket.

I appreciated the gesture, but I'd been on my own for a very long time and whatever this was, I would handle it. But inside my house, I double-checked every door and window just to be safe. Everything was locked up tight, the security system was armed and I headed upstairs to get ready for bed.

By the time my head hit the pillow, every sound I heard was a potential serial killer coming to do me in.

Tomorrow, I'd have a drink before bed.

Chapter 3

Tate

My new favorite place in all of Mayhem was my shop, GET INK'D. This time of day, when the guys were probably still sleeping from a long night of drinking and fucking at the clubhouse, the place was quiet. I was alone to survey this thing I'd built with my hands. And the government's money. Looking around the deep red chairs, the shiny chrome tattoo guns and the disinfecting station. Yep, this was all mine and no one could take it away.

As I unpacked the alcohol pads and bandages, I thought about my brother's life with Jana. They'd gone through some shit to get together, but somehow they'd come out the other side stronger and happier. Never in my life would I have imagined that lovey-dovey shit would appeal to me – marriage and ankle biters.

Hell, before I'd gone to prison I was a playboy through and through. There was a different girl, sometimes two, in my bed wherever and whenever I wanted and I was fucking proud of it. But now, that shit felt like a waste of time and I couldn't see why. I was sure some headshrinker would tell me it had to do with a need to make shit count and not waste my time since so much of it had been stolen from me.

Cross's words had pissed me off too, like I didn't want to get laid. What red-blooded man with a working cock wouldn't want to bury himself into a warm, willing cunt? But the Reckless Bitches weren't doing it for me and the last thing I wanted was to go be a freak show at a bar or restaurant. Teddy was interesting, but I couldn't shit where I ate. She was like family and that meant she was off limits.

So, it was just me and my hand, like it had been for the past six years.

And that thought made me angry all over again. I'd give anything to get over the fucking anger. It didn't help shit and I worried that it might land me back to a fucking cage. I needed to deal with it, but I couldn't bring myself to see a shrink, no matter how much Max pushed. He'd given me the number of his doctor, but I wasn't ready to bear my soul to Dr. Singh. Not yet.

The bell chimed and I looked up, a groan following nanoseconds later as one of the Reckless Bitches sauntered in wearing a skintight mini-skirt and one of those bustier tops that showed off her leathery skin from too many hours in a tanning bed. "Hey, Golden Boy," she cooed, doing her best to sound like a woman half her age.

"What do you want, Sheena?"

"You," she said, her gaze as straightforward as her words.

I sighed and clenched my fists. "I don't have time for your games. State your business or leave."

She pouted and came closer until her tits rubbed up against my arm, pushing up on the balls of her feet in an attempt to nibble my ear, but I stepped back and she nearly fell. "I'm here for you, Golden Boy. For anything you want."

I took several deep breaths and counted back from ten, the way one of the students who'd help free me had taught when my anger got the better of me. I put three feet between us and crossed my arms. "I'm not fucking around with you, Sheena."

She flicked her brown hair full of too many acid-blonde streaks behind her shoulders and closed the gap between us, sliding the tips of her fingers into the waistband of my jeans. "I said *anything*, Golden Boy. You've been locked up a long time," she began and licked her lips.

I started counting back from twenty.

"Unless, maybe you love cock now."

My hand wrapped around her wrist and pushed her back until she stumbled. "Get the fuck out of here."

"But Golden Boy," she began, long red nails sliding up and down my chest.

"I said, get the fuck out! Now! Or I swear to fuckin' God I will put you out."

She frowned, a look of hell in her brown gaze. "Damn, Tate! You used to be fun. Hot and always up for a good time. But now you're just a boring piece of shit and I'm not the only one who thinks so."

I laughed, like that was supposed to hurt my damn feelings. "Yeah and you're still the ugly bitch you always were. Now get the *fuck* out and don't come near me again!"

She gasped and hurried out, nearly bumping into Max as he pulled open the door.

Max stepped back to let Sheena pass with an amused smirk on his face. "What the hell was that about?"

I shrugged. "Same old Reckless Bitch bullshit." I smacked the wall beside me with more force than I intended, making a small dent in the wall. "Fuck! This is why the fuck I haven't been around the clubhouse. I can't get a fucking moment of peace there! Shit!"

"You need to calm down Tate or you won't be able to focus on your business. Don't let some stupid shit distract you. This is your shot. Keep your eye on the prize."

I nodded, flexing my hands to stop from punching a hole in the goddamn wall. Max was right. I had a to-do list as long as my arm. It kinda pissed me off that he had to remind me of what was important but that was why Max was the man. He had my back no matter what. Losing it over a piece of trash like Sheena? What was I thinking? She was nothing to me. But I couldn't let Max think he had the upper hand with me.

"What would you know about starting a business? Think you're my fuckin' boss now?"

"Asshole," he laughed and shook his head. "Got time for a quick tat?"

"For you? Always."

Chapter 4

Teddy

"You didn't say anything about the flowers." Kip Riley stood in front of me with a dimpled smile and his Justin Bieber hair, his hands shoved in his pocket in an effort to appear nonthreatening. His light blue eyes did their best to have that 'aw shucks' look that had made him so popular.

"What...you?" I shook my head and let out several deep breaths, curling my hands into fists until deep crescents dug into my palm. "That really was unnecessary and I don't appreciate it. At all."

One flinger slid up my arm and I smacked it away. "It's just a little gift to show you my appreciation."

And this guy was the reason I didn't dedicate more than a few hours in bed to any man. "You're paying me, and giving your bride the wedding of her dreams is enough for me. Don't ever fucking do it again." I pointed a French manicured nail between his eyes. "If you do, I'll back out at the absolute last minute. Got it?" He nodded and I turned to the producer behind the camera. "You better get it too, because I'm not fucking around with you people."

"Yeah, we all got it," the woman said and rolled her eyes. Bitch.

"Good. We're done here, so please get the fuck out and have a nice day." I flashed the smile I used at the end of every runway, which usually made people forget their good sense.

Once I was free of the camera crew, I locked up the office and jumped in my Mercedes, cranking up the air conditioning and Jay-Z, because sometimes that was what a girl needed to calm down after the slimy Kip Riley and to steel myself for my consultation with Tate. Big, blond and too charming, Tate. I wouldn't think about those searing gray blue eyes that seemed so much more intense than his brother's, and the fact that he was so big he took up all the space in every room. He was just too much damn man and I wasn't in the market for one of those, at least not for longer than a night or two.

There was a parking spot open right in front of GET INK'D, behind a red, black and chrome bike and I pulled in and took a few breaths before stepping out of the car. The window had big black gothic letters bearing the name of the shop, giving it that badass tattoo parlor feel. "Just a minute," Tate's familiar voice called out when the bell sounded over the door.

"Sure thing, I'll just look around while you finish…your afternoon self-love session, I assume." He chuckled as I looked around at the framed oversized drawings. They looked like pencil and charcoal, and they were done with a very skilled hand. "Did you do these drawings, because they are fantastic?"

He grunted, clearly in disbelief. "Don't blow smoke up my ass, darlin'. I was just starting to like you."

I jumped at his proximity, turning to him with a laugh. "I don't blow smoke except with my brides and believe me I don't want anything from you to make the effort to blow smoke. You're a talented artist. That's a fact, not a compliment." I poked my finger in his chest to punctuate my point, ignoring how hard his muscles were. Or at least trying to.

He laughed. "Glad we cleared that up. Now should we get down to business?"

"Might as well." I took a step away. "Damn, do you have a furnace under your skin?"

His deep chuckle echoed in the empty shop. "What can I say, I'm just hot as hell."

Damn straight. "Yeah, yeah. You're totally irresistible. The cat's pajamas and all that."

He frowned and motioned me toward the long red seat. "So, what you're saying is that I'm a catch in the 1940's?"

"Totally." My gaze focused on the golden, corded muscles of his forearm and I licked my lips unconsciously, totally oblivious to the pages he'd spread out before us.

"Well, what do you think?"

"I think they're damn good, Tate."

"But?"

I blinked. "But, nothing. They're really great."

Tate grunted and shook his head. "This is a tattoo, Teddy. That means its permanent so you should make damn sure you like it. Where is this art going on your body?"

My frown deepened and I wondered if he was trying to be funny. "Are you for real?"

He froze, gray eyes darkening like thunderclouds. "Yeah. Is this one of those crazy girl things where I'm just supposed to know? Because if so, I vote tramp stamp."

Damn Tate and that handsome face. "No," I sighed. "It's not that, but…shit, now I'll sound like a dick. But remember, you asked Golden Boy." He nodded and I took a deep breath. "I used to be a model, a pretty famous one actually which is why I thought you knew, not because I'm an egomaniac. Anyway, I did it all, runways in Paris and Milan, covers on every fashion magazine from Toledo to Tokyo. From the age of sixteen until about three years ago." I looked at Tate just to see his reaction. There was usually pity or disgust, both fucking pissed me off.

"Really? I mean you're hot, but you're not all stuck up like I expected a Paris and Milan model would be."

"*Former* model," I corrected him with a smile. "One day I was crossing the street on the Upper East Side, headed to a lunch meeting to be the new face of Chanel when a fucking cab jumped the curb and plowed right into me and nine other people. I took the brunt of the hit, leaving my left leg shattered in multiple places and resulting in a limp that pretty much ended my career." I let out a long, slow breath, my gaze fixed on the black and white tiled floor.

"Shit, what about like magazines and shit? Plenty of models don't have to walk." He frowned and in that moment, I liked Tate a lot more than I realized.

"You'd think that, wouldn't you?" But like me, he would have been wrong too. I lifted up the wide-leg black linen pants I wore until the whole scar — from the middle of my calf all the way up to my hip — all twenty-one inches of it, was exposed to his gaze. "I want to, not necessarily cover it but …" I trailed off, not sure how to explain it.

"Decorate it?"

I smiled. "Sure, let's go with that."

He nodded, letting out a breath of relief, probably since he hadn't been expecting such a show of emotion from me. "Okay. First, what do you need? A hug? A drink? A primal scream therapy session?"

"If I say yes to all three?"

"I'm in. Always up for two out of three of those." When he smiled like that, Tate looked like a little boy, so light and carefree. Such a contrast from the shadows he constantly wore.

"Not much of a hugger?"

He shook his head and stood. "Look at these, smartass."

I did, taking a look at the various designs. Some were vines done in a Celtic style, others were thorny vines with roses that hadn't yet bloomed and a few others were similar in theme. "This is beautiful," I said out loud as I took in the long peacock feathers.

"Take this," he said gruffly to cover up the sweet gesture of him bringing me a drink.

"Thanks, Golden Boy."

He smirked but bit back whatever comment was on the tip of his tongue. "You like the feathers?"

"I do, but I'm not sure how that can work with all this," I told him, gesturing to my leg.

Tate sat on the stool and motioned to my leg, which I laid across his lap. "I'm a fucking pro. Peacock feathers are long so we can start here," the pad of his finger began two inches below where the scar started, and I got goose bumps at his touch. "And they can fan up to here," he stopped at my hip. "What do you think?"

"You're being very *not* weird about this, Tate."

He let out an unamused laugh. "I've seen a lot worse than a long skinny scar on a great pair of legs. Honestly, your legs are more distracting than the scar."

A laugh bubbled up out of me. "That's probably the nicest thing anyone has ever said to me."

"That's me," he rolled his eyes. "Sweetest motherfucker around."

"Don't sell yourself short, Golden Boy. You'd be surprised at the shit people say to me." I took the drink and then, feeling uncomfortable, changed the subject. "How long will this take?"

"I could do it in one session if you're okay with that, otherwise it'll take two, about four hours each."

"Four hours! Each? Is this surgery?"

"Not quite, but it is art."

Right. "And art takes time. Got it. Now I have another question and I need you to promise you won't judge me."

"You wanna know how bad it hurts?"

I shook my head. "Yes and no. I want to know if it will hurt when you go over the scar tissue."

"Shit, of course. It depends on how fresh the scars are, Teddy."

To me they always felt brand new, like it happened last week, not three years ago. "Well, I guess we'll find out, won't we?"

He flashed a smile that I felt all the way down to my long neglected pussy. "As soon as you set a date."

"I'll let you know." I wanted the tattoo. I needed to get it, no matter how much time it took. Or how bad it hurt. We sat there in a comfortable silence for several long moments, me staring at the peacock feathers and imagining the end result. Tate stared at the tiles, lost in his own thoughts. "So, can I ask you a question without you getting your panties in a twist?"

He grinned, looking every inch the big, tough, biker he was. "Guess it's a good thing I left my panties at home."

That was another thing I liked about Tate, he didn't take things too seriously. "Self-defense. What do you know about it?"

"Uncle Sam taught me to fight. Hand to hand combat, plus a little martial arts. I can help you. If you can help me."

I stiffened, ready to slice him open with my tongue as soon as he made the inappropriate comment.

"Calm down, Teddy. I want you to help me plan a wedding for Max and Jana. That's your thing, isn't it?"

Damn, I was right back to liking him. "Yeah sure, I can help you with that. But be prepared for details. Lots and lots of details. Okay?"

He nodded. "Thanks."

"No problems. Thanks for the awesome artwork, Golden Boy."

He grinned. "Anytime, Cover Girl."

I smiled as I left the shop because when he said those words, it didn't feel like a reminder of who I used to be. It just felt...amazing.

***

"So you want the cornflower napkins and roses to match?" To me, it sounded like the tackiest shit I'd ever heard, but it wasn't my wedding.

"That's right. I found the most adorbs cornflower blue lingerie and it totally matches Kip's eyes, don'tcha think?" Gillian Frye, most recent winner of *I Wanna Fall in Love*, gushed over her slimy groom to be.

"Sure. And you still want Elvis to marry you?"

She nodded, bleach blonde ponytail bobbing up and down. "My dad *loves* Elvis and he'd never be able to afford this kind of wedding, so this is kind of for him."

"I have a few in mind, do you want to audition them?"

Her green eyes went round and wide. "We can do that?" She looked from me to the producer behind the camera.

"Sure, it'll be great for the show!"

I rolled my eyes as Gillian popped up and sauntered off, her mute by choice bestie tottering after her in matching bubblegum pink heels. "I guess we're done here," I mumbled to myself, ignoring the camera aimed at my hands since I refused to sign a consent form to be filmed. "You guys can go now."

"Why would we do that?" Kip asked as he appeared from the smaller office used by my assistants. "I've been looking forward to seeing you again." I stood as he came closer because I wasn't a fool. It was a hard lesson, but being trapped in a room with one too many pervy photographers and grabby male models had taught me to be aware.

"Well the meeting is over, so you can all be gone." I made a *shooing* motion that only made the bastard smile. He let his finger trail up and down my arm, laughing when I smacked his hand away. "Keep your fucking hands to yourself, Kip."

He grinned again and stepped closer, I pushed him and he stumbled. "Come on, babe. No need to play hard to get." He did a quick spin and was steady on his feet wearing a shit-eating grin.

Behind my desk I kept a bat. A big aluminum bat that I reached for and smacked the edge of my desk. "Touch me again motherfucker and I swear to God I'll quit. I will fucking walk away and leave you to do this yourself. Got it?" He nodded, his smile gone as he held his hands up defensively. "Got it?" I asked the producer too. The last fucking thing I needed was to have the bride labeling me a home wrecker on national TV.

"Yeah, we got it."

"Good. Now get the fuck out of my office and don't come back without the bride." When they were gone, I locked the door and let out a long, tense breath. Kip was an asshole and that producer chick was a fucking prick, but I didn't throat punch anyone so to me, today was a complete success.

And since my day was over, I kicked out the last two assistants and locked the place up for the night. I picked up some sushi and a bottle of gin before heading home.

Where another damn package sat on my porch. I took a few deep breaths and got out of the car, phone in hand as I approached. It was a ticking bomb, I knew that, but who knew with Kip? The box was pink and white, almost like Victoria's Secret but not quite. Inside was trashy, lacy lingerie, and it was shredded to pieces.

A fucking threat if I ever saw one, so I called the police. Which I immediately regretted.

"What seems to be the problem ma'am?" The uniformed officer was blond and looked to be about sixteen years old.

"Are you kidding? Someone sent me shredded lingerie! No, not *sent*, apparently they dropped it off."

His partner snickered and I glared at them both. "Perhaps an angry lover?"

"Doubtful since I don't have a lover and if I did, he wouldn't know where I live. I don't play that game." I never brought men home and the house was in my old name, so it wasn't easy to find. "Am I to understand from your little girl giggles that you're not going to do anything about it?"

"Not much we can do," the blond one said, still trying to stifle a laugh.

"Thank you for fuck all. But if I end up dead, you'll have to live with it." His face paled. "Thanks for nothing, officers. Goodbye." So angry, I shook. I slammed the door before they even turned around to leave.

Why did I call the cops? Not one time in my life have they ever come through for me. Not when my mom was dying of an overdose right in front of me, because they "didn't have gloves." Not later when a foster brother got a little too close, because of course being in foster care somehow means you're defective or promiscuous. And certainly not when my last foster dad tried to take what didn't belong to him. They were as useless as tits on a bicycle, so it was up to me to protect myself.

I promised to call Tate soon for those self-defense lessons, but first I sat down and began to research gun laws in the state of Nevada.

Chapter 5

Tate

"So, you're like a real life biker?" A tiny little blonde flirted with me, leaning so far over the counter I could damn near see the tops of her nipples.

"I own a bike, if that's what you mean." I smiled at her even though I wasn't interested, because being *not* interested pissed me the fuck off. She was exactly the kind of girl I could get my cock wet with and leave without a look back. But I didn't want her. "You like bikes?"

"I've been on one before and all that power between my legs . . ." She shivered and squealed instead of finishing the thought.

"Yeah? Well my boy Dallas loves nothing more than giving a pretty girl a ride on the back of his bike. Lasso," I called to the big, blonde Texan.

Her brows crinkled adorably and it was then I realized she couldn't be more than twenty. "Why do you call him Lasso?"

Because the man roped more tail than ten cowboys. "Because he's a real life cowboy, darlin'." Her eyes went wide as Dallas strode over, jeans tight and black t-shirt even tighter under his *kutte.* He flashed a dimpled grin and raked a hand through curly blond hair as he stopped in front of her, damn near casting a shadow over her petite frame.

"Howdy, darlin'. What's your name?"

She giggled and put her tiny hand in his. "I'm Marcy, and you're a real life cowboy!"

Lasso flashed a smile at me and winked down at her. "Well I was one, until Uncle Sam needed my help." And just like that, Marcy's panties were probably soaked through. "You done shootin', sugar? I was thinking about taking a sunset ride on my bike."

"Want some company?"

"When the company looks like you, damn straight."

I laughed as he looped her arm around his gigantic ass bicep and walked away. He winked over his shoulder at me and I rolled my eyes. Some shit never changed, and for once, I was glad of it. Fucking Lasso.

A few older women stopped by the gun range desk, looking for help loading up a couple Desert Eagles, flirtatious but only because I was young and buff. It was easy to be around women like that because they just wanted a young buck to make them feel sexy and I could do that in my sleep. "Thank you, handsome."

"Anytime, beautiful." She blushed and they giggled like schoolgirls as I walked away. "Gunnar, what's up man?" I hadn't seen our VP since I started spending more time at the clubhouse, which was shitty because we used to be close.

"Just got back from Denver. Had to put my ma in a home. Fucking Alzheimer's."

"Shit man, sorry to hear that. How's she doing?"

He laughed bitterly. "Better than me because she has no fucking clue what's going on most of the time." His shoulders dropped and he raked a hand through his thick, dark hair. "If shit was different I could keep her with me, but...fuck!"

"She needs around the clock care, Gun. Even if you didn't have the Reckless Bastards, you'd have to work somewhere at least eight hours a day." I knew that shit firsthand. With Max off on missions he couldn't talk about, I'd been forced to put mom in a home when she showed early signs of dementia. But she'd died while he was in the desert and I was rotting in prison.

"Shit man, I didn't even think."

I held up a hand to stop the apology I didn't need or fucking want. "Don't worry, I'm just telling you how it is. Visit her often and it'll be as easy as it's ever gonna be."

"Thanks, Golden Boy. How are you—"

Savior strolled up looking like he'd just been butt fucked by the devil, and all of that anger was aimed my way. "What the fuck, Golden Boy? Sheena said you got rough with her!"

Of course that no good bitch said that. I got in his face the same way he was in mine. Savior was a crazy bastard, but I was angry, bigger than him by at least four inches and fifty pounds of muscle because the only fucking thing I did over the past six years was read and weight train.

"Sheena needs to learn to keep her fucking hands to herself! I didn't do shit to her other than remove her hands from *my fucking body!*" Fear flashed in his eyes, but Savior was no punk and he held his ground. I would've been impressed if I wasn't so damn mad. "Thanks for the vote of fucking confidence, man. If you're so worried about the bitch, make her your old lady."

The crazy fucker smiled and grabbed my shoulder. "Fuck that shit. That girl is a first-class bunny boiler over there. I'm just checkin' in with you man, you're wound tighter than a virgin's asshole."

I shook my head at his foolishness. "You're still a crazy sonofabitch, you know that?"

"All part of my charm, brother. You know I'd never doubt you, right? Well I doubt any man who hasn't wet his dick with a willing woman after years of abstinence, but other than that, we're brothers, asshole."

"Yeah, I know. I need to get my head on straight, first."

"All right, how about we go for a ride this week?"

A smile spread across my face. "Sounds good, Savior. Name the day and time."

"I want some new ink, schedule me last and we'll go after?" He didn't wait for an answer, just fist bumped me and Gunnar, and walked off whistling.

I looked to Gunnar. "I gotta get to the shop man, later." Walking through the parking lot, I couldn't help the goofy as grin I wore. For the first time since I got out, I felt like I was home again.

With my family.

***

"Hey, Tate. Come on in. Thanks for coming." She was stiff, wooden and on edge.

"No problem. Hey, you okay Teddy?"

She blinked, jumping and gasping when I touched her shoulder. "Yeah, I'm fine. Why do you ask?"

I grinned. "Honey you're jumpy as hell. Tell me what's going on?"

She sighed and turned to me, her tumble of red hair falling around her shoulder, vibrant and beautiful. "Don't freak out, okay?"

"I'm a man, Teddy. We don't freak out."

She rolled her eyes and clasped our hands together as she pulled me through her split-level home, barely giving me a chance to take it all in. "Yeah right. You forgot I've seen Max in action." There was a hint of sarcasm there, but her voice was still tense as we entered the backyard. "Remember you promised not to freak out."

"I didn't, but okay." She turned to me and stepped aside, pushing open the door to a little storage shed at the back corner of her garage.

"Well, look!" She gestured to the open door and I stepped inside.

"What the fuck?"

She nibbled her lip, another sign that whatever was going on had her spooked. "Someone has been sending me gifts. No, not *someone*. I think it's this groom for the wedding I'm working on. He's a slime ball, always hitting on me."

"Why do you think this is him?" I listened as she told me, in a shaky voice, about the flowers and candy. "That's not quite the same as torn lingerie and slashed photos of you, I'm assuming from your modeling days?" Had to be because she was young, gorgeous and not a redhead. "You're a natural blonde?"

She laughed. "No. I dyed it blonde because everyone wanted a blonde. The red is natural." She grabbed a handful, lifted it up and let it fall to her shoulders.

"Well. Red does match your fiery as shit personality." She scowled and I laughed. "So, I guess self-defense first and wedding stuff, second?"

She nodded and gave me a grateful smile. "Thanks, Tate." Teddy shook her head, a frown forming on her face. "Who in the hell would want to stalk a mangled former model?"

"Mangled? Are you fucking blind on top of everything else?"

She stopped and glared at me. "I know what I look like Tate, but I'm nobody anymore."

"We're all somebody, Teddy."

She shook her head, about ten seconds from breaking down. "I'm sorry about this, I didn't mean to dump it all over you. I need a drink." She marched back to her kitchen, pulled out a half-empty bottle of gin and poured a shot. "Shit! Why did I do that?"

I laughed and took the bottle. "Take a seat." Her kitchen was organized, making it easy to find what I needed. Tonic water and a grapefruit. "Here."

"Thanks." She took several long gulps, draining half the glass. "Okay, let's just do wedding stuff. I'm going to get a gun."

"You know that you're more likely to be killed with your own gun?"

She nodded and took another sip. "And I'll definitely end up dead if I *don't* get one, Golden Boy. Do you think this will stop at gifts? I don't. A girl I modeled with ended up dead thanks to a guy she smiled at in line at a coffee shop. He thought they were building something and when she disagreed, he broke in to her apartment and choked her to death."

There was more she didn't say and I didn't ask. Prying wasn't my thing. But I could help. "The club has a gun range and it's open to the public. Come by and I'll teach you how to shoot."

"To kill, right?"

I laughed. "You always shoot to kill."

"Good to know. Now, tell me Golden Boy, have you been dreaming of your brother's wedding since you were a little boy?"

"You really are a smartass."

"Yeah, tell me something I don't know. Tell me Tate, do you have any idea what they want for this wedding?"

"Honestly? No. But I want to do this for them. You know Jana, couldn't you just do some down low recon?" When she threw her head back and laughed, my body tightened in response. Heat coursed through my veins and my cock began to swell, which was no fucking good. This was Teddy. Sure she was hot as fuck with that wavy red hair and long, shapely legs. Never mind that sharp tongue of hers. But she was best friends with my future sister-in-law. "Shit."

"You okay?"

Fuck no I wasn't okay. "Yeah, I'm fine. So, you'll talk to Jana?"

"No. You will. Take her out to lunch and ask her how the planning is going. I promise she'll talk your ear off and all you have to do is remember it all."

"That's it? Easy peasy."

"Lemon squeeze-y," she shot back and stole my untouched glass. "Fill me up, barkeep."

I made more drinks while she grabbed her tablet and began typing like a fiend. "I'll find out the date they want to tie the knot and then we can look for venues. And don't even say your clubhouse."

I frowned and turned to her. "You got something against the club?"

"Christ you're a touchy one, aren't you? I don't know shit about bikers other than what romance novels and Kurt Sutter tells me. But I know that some of your guys weren't nice to her and she's not comfortable around them. She'll handle it because she loves Max, but even at your grand opening, she was uncomfortable."

Shit. "How come I didn't know this?"

She shrugged. "Max handled it. Plus, it happened while you were fighting for your freedom and shit."

I liked how she made light of it, unlike everyone else who whispered it like it was cancer. "That should be my next tattoo, 'Freedom & Shit.'"

She nodded her agreement. "Right across your neck, like this," she gestured a throat-cutting move that made me laugh.

"That's like foreshadowing a future where I end up back in prison."

"Or," she held up a finger, shoulders squared with a knowing look on her face, "it's how people expect a guy who owns a tattoo shop to look." She shrugged. "Or we could go with your way," she added sarcastically.

"So, how'd you meet Jana?"

"We met at a support group for trauma victims. The group sucked and we gave it up, but the friendship stuck."

"She's great for Max. I think I might like having a sister. I wanted one for a while just so I could have someone to boss around. Didn't happen, though."

"She's the best sister I've ever had and believe me I've had a few."

I didn't know what the hell that meant, but it sounded like a longer conversation than I wanted to have right now. "Then I guess I owe Max."

"Giving him a wedding is great payback. So, we both have homework for next time."

I groaned. "Homework? Now *I* need a damn drink."

She laughed and pushed her glass toward me. "Drink up, I'll order food to soak it up so you don't fall off that death-cycle of yours."

"That sounds good. Thanks, Cover Girl."

She glared. "You're not that cute, Tate."

I laughed at her attempt to look tough. "I'll bet you think you look real tough, don't you?" She stuck her chin out defiantly.

"As tough as Tinker Bell, honey." She glared and picked up her phone. "Whatever we get, let's make it extra spicy with lots of anchovies."

I patted my rock hard belly. "Mmm, my favorite."

"Oh shut up and make us another drink. This time, put a little alcohol in it, will ya?"

"Be careful what you ask for, honey." I added double shots to both glasses and she nodded her approval while she placed the order at a Chinese joint. This was one weird ass night, but it was the most normal I'd felt in a long damn time.

Chapter 6

Teddy

"Holy shit, this feels amazing!" I laughed, probably a lot louder than necessary but with the protective headgear and all the shooting, I felt half deaf. "I didn't hit anything, but damn that's powerful!"

Tate laughed and lifted up one of the headphones. "You have to aim if you want to hit anything besides trees, Cover Girl." He ducked when I threw both hands in the air, gun waving like a flag. "Hey. Don't ever wave a loaded gun around. Rule number one, okay?"

"Shit, my bad. Yes. Got it. No waving a gun around like I just don't care." I flashed a toothy grin at him. "Seriously, sorry."

"Now you know and you won't forget it."

"Definitely not with the death stare you just sent my way," I told him as I squared my shoulders and turned toward the target. "Now help me kill something."

"You're gonna have to spread those legs."

Oh fuck. I wasn't ashamed to admit that I shivered when his big, warm body pressed behind me, his rough hands sliding down my arms to make sure my elbows were just right when I held the gun. "I'll bet you say that to all the girls."

His deep chuckle rumbled behind me, rattling my spine but I kept my shoulders squared and back straight. Just because Tate was a hot piece of man didn't mean I needed to hand over my panties. "Funny."

I looked over my shoulder at him and, holy shit, I really shouldn't have. The man had that whole rugged outlaw biker sex appeal on a good day, but when he smiled my panties just...incinerated. "I can be," I told him and spread my legs. "This good?"

His hands skimmed my hips. "A little more, but keep your hips squared and bend your knees just a bit. Drop this elbow," he told me, his hand once again gliding over the area in question. "All right, now the gun shouldn't knock you on your pretty little ass."

I wiggled for good measure. "I did feel kind of unsteady before. Maybe I shouldn't shoot in stilettos?"

"No, you definitely should." His voice was thick with desire and lightly flirtatious. "Maybe we should do a half-off deal for girls in bikinis and heels."

I laughed. "Now that's a good marketing plan, Golden Boy." I snorted a laugh. "Hey you could be one of The Outsiders, remember that movie? Shit, I haven't thought about that in forever."

"The Outsiders? That old ass movie with Tom Cruise?"

"One and the same. You could've been Pony Boy's brother or his cousin from out of town," I told him, barely able to contain my laughter.

"Are you obsessed with that movie or something," he asked and stepped back so I could line up my shot.

"Nope. One of the foster homes I stayed in, the parents were always gone and they would lock us in the basement with tons of VHS tapes. My favorite was The

Outsiders." I waited for the pity or some trite remark, but the fucker laughed. Laughed!

"Don't tell me, you discovered yourself as a woman to that film?"

This time I put the gun down and doubled over with laughter. "Oh, Tate. Who knew you were such a funny fucker?"

He shrugged. "I'm an acquired taste."

"Hmph," was all I could reply because my mind rolled a few images I had no business thinking about. I got myself under control and picked the gun back up, whispering each step to myself. "And squeeze," I said and pulled the trigger. My eyes whipped open and I squinted. "Oh shit, I actually hit it!" I jumped up and down, wrapping an arm around Tate. "Die fucker!"

Tate chuckled and shook his head. "All right, Annie Oakley, let's see if you can do it again."

I did. Again and again. Mostly my bullets clipped the outer edge of the paper, nowhere near the human silhouette, but it felt damn good. "So in about two years, I'll be ready to protect myself," I told him an hour later.

"Nah, you'll be ready way sooner. But you need to do this a few more times. I'll even give you a discount for the open carry class. It's six classes but you'll know how to shoot, clean and load your weapon. Plus, overall safety."

I couldn't help but grin. "Look at you, being all business-like."

He grinned and rolled his eyes. "Quiet, Cover Girl, let me show you what to do next." Tate stood close, showing me how to check the chamber without shooting myself in the face. "We'll do cleaning next time."

"Eager to get rid of me?"

"Hell yeah. I hate beautiful women who smell good. Yuck," he added with a shiver.

"Whatever." I shoulder checked him as we went inside so I could pay for today's lesson. I insisted.

"Thanks for this Tate, I'm no safer but I don't feel so…victimized."

"That's a start. Just call for your next lesson."

I nodded, grabbed my purse and walked through the elaborate structure that finally spit me out onto the blacktop parking lot. I slid my Chanel glasses down to shield my eyes. I loved these sunglasses, they were classics and they were the first major purchase I'd made with a modeling check. It had been a fantastic feeling and the fact they were still in one piece made me feel like less of an asshole for dropping so much cash on a pair of sunglasses. Though here in sunny Nevada, they got a lot more use than when I was based in New York.

"Hey bitch, just because you *used* to be somebody don't mean you can come in here and take what don't belong to ya!" A stringy-haired blonde with bad highlights and high-waisted acid washed jeans stopped right in my path. She was a little shorter and a little rounder than me, but she looked mean as a junkyard dog. "Fucking slut."

"Look bitch, I don't know who you think you are but if you have a problem you should probably take it up with the dick that's got you acting like a damn fool, and not me. Because I'm not in the fucking mood." I could tell I shocked her and I was damn proud of that. People, especially women, thought they could intimidate me because they didn't know that I was a bitch on wheels with just enough hell in me to make them regret it. "And while you're at it, you should get those split ends checked out." I skirted past her and kept walking toward my car, feeling a little amped up by the encounter with the eighties barfly.

"Stay away or I'll make you pay, bitch!" she screamed and seconds later I felt air whizz by my head as a beer bottle sailed past me.

"Learn how to throw, hooker!" I laughed and unlocked my car with my key fob as I approached it, shaking my head at the foolish woman. Why was it that women always wanted to fight over the one thing in this world that didn't mean shit? Men, yeah right. My career, Jana, my life…yes. Men weren't even worth the effort of balling up my fist.

And definitely not the bruised and bloodied knuckles, because I didn't slap. I jabbed.

I refused to let that woman ruin my good mood and decided to head to Jana's house. Maybe some alcohol therapy and girl time would make me feel better about everything. I parked behind her Prius and walked around the back because it was a nice day and Jana loved her backyard. I found her staring off into space like something was terribly wrong. "What's up? Is it Max? Do we need to kill him or something, because I will totally be your alibi."

Jana turned to me with tears swimming in her eyes but slowly enough to torture me, her mouth pulled up into a grin. "Nothing as bad as all that. Teddy, I'm pregnant."

I gasped at the idea that I'd have a little niece or nephew to spoil rotten, then a frown appeared. "Oh, I get it. You're in love with a big handsome man who thinks the world was created just for you, an awesome career and the bestest best friend ever. Your life totally sucks."

She smacked me playfully. "Shut up."

"You're happy about this. Right?"

Jana nodded, flicking her long blonde hair out of her face as she sniffled. "I am, Teddy. I really, really am. It's just, well I'd given up on thinking this would ever happen for me, you know? And what if Max isn't happy?"

I shook my head and smacked my lips, giving her a *what the hell* look. "You know Jana, doctors frown on pregnant women smoking crack."

"Teddy," she whined.

"Look, Max thinks the sun shines out of your pussy. He'll be so happy that he's probably going to smother you with love and overprotectiveness. You'll be wrapped so tight in cotton that you'll want to kill him before you even start showing." She laughed and I wrapped my arms around her. "Seriously, you should probably jump up and down, maybe run up the steps two at a time and carry a big box before he finds out."

Jana's body shook with laughter and I felt better too. "Thank you, Teddy."

"Don't worry. I love you and you're going to be an amazing mother, trust me."

"Teddy," she began nervously. "What if...what if my face scares my baby?"

My heart instantly broke for Jana. Not because of the jagged scar on the right side of her face, but because she really didn't see how incredible she was. "That's never going to happen. You'll love that little tyke so much, take such good care of it that it'll think something is wrong with the other moms who don't have a hero mark."

"Oh, Teddy," she cried and then sobbed so hard her body shook.

"Well now that you're already a blubbering mess, I think I should tell you about something." I sucked in a deep breath and put a few feet of distance between us as I finally told her all about the gifts. "They started a while ago. I think it's Kip Riley."

"Teddy, you have to call the cops."

I scoffed. "Yeah, I did that and they were no fucking help at all. Laughed, if you can believe it." That still made me angry enough to cause bodily harm, but it wasn't worth it so I shrugged it off.

"Teddy," she began but I held up my hands to stop her.

"I'm doing all that can be done, Jana. Don't worry about me and please, don't tell Max." She hesitated but I looked right through her. "Please."

She nodded. "As long as you're not in any danger, I won't say a word."

"That's good enough for me." For now, anyway. I didn't want Max getting involved and especially not now, with a kid on the way. "It'll be fine, don't worry." I would worry enough for the both of us.

She listened as I told her about the randomness and over all sexual tone of the gifts, nodding as her gaze was set on a fixed point in the distance. "You should stay with us."

"Yeah, right. Because I want to catch you christening every part of this place? No thanks, but thank you for the offer. Besides, you and Max are still getting used to living together."

"It's been six months," she reminded me with a roll of her eyes.

"Still. You'll be nesting, or whatever, soon. I'll be fine and even if I'm not, there's no way I'm putting you in the vicinity of harm's way."

I groaned when Jana began to tear up again. "You are too good to me, Teddy. I love you."

"I love you too, honey. Now you need to go rinse that face and put on something sexy when you tell Max he's gonna be a daddy. There's a bottle of wine at home calling my name."

And thankfully no gifts waiting for me when I got there.

Chapter 7

Tate

Running my shop was easier than I'd thought it would be. Hell, getting the paperwork done for a business license had been harder, plus all the health and safety shit the state *and* the city required. The job itself was easy — scheduling the guys, booking appointments and disinfecting between customers — but the days were still long with inventory logs and bookkeeping. As I closed up late on a Friday evening, I started to think that maybe I should take Jana up on her offer to help.

I knew I wouldn't, not yet anyway. So far none of it was too difficult, just time consuming as fuck. But it's not like I had a lot to keep me busy other than GET INK'D and the Reckless Bastards. Sad fucking life, but I wasn't ready to do much more yet. Prison life was very regimented and even if I hadn't needed that kind of structure, it stuck with me. Some guys had gotten out and come back in less than a year because freedom made them go buck wild and they ended up right back in a cage. I refused to let that shit happen to me.

No. Fucking. Way.

I'd just finished locking up when I felt a pair of hands grab me from behind. Instantly my instincts kicked in. Six years of being locked up with murderers, rapists and con men, I learned not to let anyone get the jump on me. I turned quickly, grabbing the asshole by the throat and slamming him against the steel gate. Only it wasn't a him. I blinked at the familiar blonde-streaked brown hair and growled. "Sheena? What the fuck, I could've fucking killed you." Fucking woman had no sense of self-preservation, did she? "I'm sure I told you to stay away from me."

She stuttered as I let go of her and took a few steps back, shoving my hands into the pockets of my jeans. "I-I'm sorry, Golden Boy. I just wanted to come see if you wanted to go to my place and order a pizza."

"I don't."

Her lips shifted to a pout as she crossed her arms, doing her best to bring her tits to my attention. "Why?"

It seemed the Reckless Bitches had gotten bolder in my absence and I didn't fucking appreciate it. "Because I don't want to, that's why."

Hurt flashed in her eyes for about a second before it turned to anger. Arms once propping up her tits shifted to her hips as she leaned forward to glare at me. "It's that hoity-toity redheaded bitch, ain't it? She's no more special than the rest of us, ya know."

"Goddammit, Sheena," I roared and took a step forward, checking myself when she took a wary step back. "What, or who, I do is none of your fucking business. Get that shit through your thick skull or next time, I won't be so nice."

She stumbled back and I took a few more steps away from her as a middle-aged couple walked by the front window. "You wouldn't know fun if it ran up and kicked you in the nuts."

I laughed, shook my head and walked toward my bike that was parked out front. Jumping on my bike to put some distance between us, I decided I wasn't ready to head back to an empty house. Now that Max and Jana were basically living together at Jana's, the house felt bigger and emptier. Like another cage holding me in. I passed a noodle shop and figured being surrounded by strangers was better than being surrounded by silence. I didn't know what the hell a noodle shop was, but I suspected some type of Asian based on the décor.

"Table for one?" a very petite Asian woman asked and I nodded. "Big man needs big table," she offered with a pat of my arm in a maternal way that reminded me of my mom.

"Thanks," I told her and stopped at a familiar halo of red hair. "Cover Girl?"

Teddy looked up and smiled. "Tate, fancy meeting you here." She gestured for me to join her and the older woman smiled as she set the menu at the empty seat.

"I'll get you a place setting," she said with authority. "Drink?"

"Beer. Something dark and creamy." She smiled, nodded and walked away.

I took the seat and drank Teddy in. She was always dressed up but tonight she had on jeans and a plain black t-shirt that still made her look like sex on stilettos. I inhaled and it felt like fire invaded my nose and eyes. "Holy hell woman, is that how you keep your body so hot, just scorching off the extra calories?" That shit in her bowl had to be illegal.

Her head fell back, sending a cascade of waves across her shoulders as she laughed. "Nah. I just have a major noodle addiction and these are so fucking spicy there's no way I can pig out on spring rolls and dumplings too."

My eyes must have bugged out my head at the way she laughed.

"You can eat that much?"

She nodded. "Oh yeah, which is why I limit myself to the spicy noodles *or* the other stuff."

"Worried about getting fat? Because from here it looks like that's a long way away."

Her smile softened. "Thanks, but the truth is that I just don't want to gain so much that I have to get rid of the clothes I've gathered over the years. They're nice and these days I only splurge on shoes, handbags and jeans."

I barked out a laugh and picked up the just delivered beer. "What else is there?"

She rolled her eyes with an affectionate smile. "Men. You know nothing of fashion."

"You wound me," I deadpanned.

"You'll live, Golden Boy." She shook her head. "I love that name."

Her glee was interrupted when the older woman, May, according to the name on her shirt, came to take my order. I ordered a bowl of seafood and noodles, plus a bit of the *other stuff* out of pure curiosity. "Now Teddy, tell me something about yourself."

"Like?" While she waited for me to specify, she used her chopsticks perfectly to scoop noodles in her mouth, totally unconcerned with the drops on her chin until she was done chewing.

Staring at her like this, dressed down and indulging in her favorite food, it occurred to me that she was as real as she was beautiful. Teddy didn't try to be tough or sexy, she just was. She was able to laugh at herself without demeaning herself, and she spoke her mind. A rare trait in women in my experience. "Why did you grow up in foster care?"

"Straight to it then, huh?" She dabbed her mouth with her napkin, as ladylike as you please, then smiled to show she wasn't bothered by my question. "My mom overdosed on heroin one times too many and when she died there was no one. She hadn't spoken to her family in years, changed her name and moved a dozen times, so it was easier for the state to put me in the system rather than actually try to track them down."

Damn. "Did you have one family or were you like Jana?"

She scoffed. "Yeah, that was one of the things that bonded us. Our inability to find a family. Now it's your turn."

I shrugged and told her all about our mom. "She was the best. Tough as hell but tender and all mom-like, you know? The woman couldn't cook a bird to save her life, but she was absolute magic with potatoes. And she was so proud of Max, then me for enlisting." Just thinking about Mom made my chest tighten, tears sting my eyes.

"It must've killed her to see you locked up," she said with no pity, just sincerity.

"It would have, but she died before that shit storm swept in." I shook my head, hearing the bitterness in my words. "She was everything to us, both of us, and yet we let some fucking war keep us away when she needed us the most. There was no one to fight for her, to make sure she got the care she deserved." That shit still ate at me even though I'd stopped thinking about it about eighteen months into what turned out to be six long as fuck years. "At first I just tried not to think of her when I was locked up because it made me angry and that's a sure-fire way to get dead or a life sentence. Then, it just made me sad."

Her smile came softly as she looked at me. "And I guess being sad in there would have been even worse?"

"Damn straight. Would've gotten me killed or fucked."

She barked out a laugh and covered her mouth. "Sorry, I probably shouldn't laugh at that, but holy shit Tate, that's funny." She smacked the table as she hiccupped with laughter.

"Glad to amuse you."

Eventually she settled down and stole one of what was supposed to be a spring roll but it didn't look like any I'd ever seen. "Tell me about how you came to be in a motorcycle club."

I frowned. "First tell me what the fuck this is," I said pointing to what looked like a bunch of grass wrapped in cellophane.

She laughed again and I was really starting to like that husky laugh that came so easily. "It's a Vietnamese spring roll, filled with rice noodles, shrimp, cucumber, basil and carrots. Try it, they're delicious," she assured me as she dipped it in a little bowl of brown sauce and took a big bite.

Fuck me, she was right as my mouth exploded in a million flavors, all of them delicious. "Damn that is good."

"Told you. Now answer up."

"It's nothing dramatic. I came out here after I left the Army in search of a path forward and found Cross and some of the other guys instead. Most of them are vets and we clicked. Max was still in the service doing off-the-books shit for Uncle Sam and Mom was gone. They became my family."

Talking to Teddy was easy, I realized. She flirted but there wasn't any intent behind it, and she asked good questions.

"Do you miss the Army?"

"Sometimes, but I like being my own boss."

"Amen to that." She grinned and took a steamed dumpling, moaning as she chewed. "You are evil for ordering these goodies." She pushed it all closer to me and I laughed.

"Fine by me, this shit is good."

"How's the inking business?"

"Going good. When do you plan to come in?"

"As soon as I get enough time to get it done."

I smiled. She was tough but I could see how she struggled with covering up the scars. They were a big part of her life, even though she hated them. Covering them would be a big change. "Come on, I'll follow you home."

"He said creepily," she said with an uneasy grin, handing May a card as she rushed past us. "Sure, I'll let you play my white knight. Or *golden* knight."

"Smart ass."

"Thank you," she said sweetly, smiling up at May as she brought a receipt for Teddy to sign. "May, as usual you have filled my tummy to perfection."

"We always love to fatten you up, Teddy. Still too skinny."

Her skin flushed pink as she looked up at me. "See why I love it here? Flattery and phenomenal food."

"Make sure she gets home safe," May said to me, a serious expression that made me wonder if she knew what had been going on with Teddy.

"Of course," I told her and asked for the check.

"Already paid," she told me with a bright smile before she hurried off.

"You paid for my meal? Hell, I don't know whether to be insulted or impressed. The only woman who ever paid for my food was my mom."

"Are we going to argue about this, Golden Boy?"

"Nope. Come on." She took my arm and let me walk her to her fancy ass car. It was simple but expensive. "I'll bet this thing rides like a dream."

"Be my designated driver one night and I'll let you find out," she said before I closed the door with a laugh.

Why did Teddy have to be so close to the only two people *I* was close to? She was gorgeous, sexy and a good fucking time. And completely off limits. With that unsatisfying thought, I hopped on my bike and followed her winding path back to the residential part of Mayhem to her house.

"Thanks," she called out as she walked up the stone path that led to her front door, but I kept an eye on her, noticing immediately when her steps slowed and then stopped.

I was off my bike and at her side in a split second, staring at the same sick shit that had turned Teddy's pale skin ghost white. "What the fuck?"

An old headshot of Teddy hung from a cleaver buried deep into her front door. "Watch your back bitch," it said in blood red paint.

Teddy began to shake and I wrapped her in my arms, calling the police with my free hand. This shit was getting out of hand, and Teddy needed more protection than she realized, which was how I ended up sleeping in her girly guestroom.

***

There was a soft woman wrapped around me and I groaned, snuggling deeper into the smooth skin and flower-scented hair. My hand went to a long, lean thigh draped over my own and I enjoyed it, sliding my hand up and down. The feel of a woman was something I'd missed for years and this woman was soft, silky-fucking-smooth. And moaning.

My eyes snapped open, trying to focus and figure out where the fuck I was. I'd had just a beer at the noodle house and some fucking wine with Teddy after the cops had left. Shit...Teddy. My gaze shifted to the right, and sure enough she was there with her arms and a leg wrapped around me, her head lying on my chest. And I didn't hate it.

I kind of liked it.

A lot.

Teddy groaned again as she started to wake up, back arched as she stretched, giving me a view of round tits with rock hard nipples that made my mouth water. I should have looked away. Hell, I should have just gotten up and gone to the bathroom, but I didn't. I just laid there and stared at her. Her tank top rode up, giving me a glimpse of a strip of skin that was still pale but with a slight tan, but her tits held me captive.

"Enjoying the view," she asked with a husky voice, still groggy from sleep.

"Fuck yeah, I am. I'm alive, aren't I?"

She rolled her eyes. "Flatterer."

"I'm just speaking the truth, Teddy." I swear her nipples beaded even tighter under my gaze and my cock stirred to life. "But it might be best if you backed away."

She smiled as she looked down at the tent in the sheet. "Damn, Golden Boy."

I chuckled at her incredulous tone, but my cock was hard as a steel rod. "Enjoying the view?"

She licked her lips and her hand reached out, stroking me through the sheet. "Mmm-hmm."

"Teddy!" I grunted at her touch but she ignored me, fascinated.

"You're big," she said, giving me a squeeze. "And thick."

"I'm a man, Teddy."

She stopped but her grip didn't loosen. "And this is a bad idea."

"Very bad," I agreed.

"The worst," she agreed with a smile in her eyes, hand still gripping my cock. "Too bad. It could've been fun," she said, releasing me and rolling off the bed. I watched her ass, in nothing but cotton pajama shorts that gave me a glimpse of the shadows beneath her ass cheeks.

"It would've been damn fun," I told her confidently.

She turned at the doorway, wearing a wistful smile. "Thanks for last night, Tate. I appreciate it."

"You're welcome, Cover Girl."

"Take a shower and I'll whip you up something to eat." Her gaze lingered on my bare chest and my still hard cock looking like a tent under the sheet. Licking her lips, she shook her head.

"That eager to get rid of me?"

"No, but it's ten and I figured you had to open the shop at some point today. Unless the key is to *not* make any money?" Her lips twitched for a long time before the laughter broke as I sent a pillow sailing toward her. Teddy ducked out of the way at the last minute. "Chop, chop."

When I was sure the little temptress was gone, I rushed to the bathroom, turning the water on cold to get rid of my hard on. When that didn't work, I took care of business like I usually did, cursing myself for turning down a hot as fuck woman who was clearly interested in my dick. "Dumbass," I grumbled before stepping out, feeling satisfied but desperate for more.

For Teddy.

No matter how bad an idea it was.

And it was a bad fucking idea.

Chapter 8

Teddy

Days later and I still couldn't stop thinking about how hard and tempting Tate felt in my hand, and I knew I was in trouble. I wanted him; specifically, I wanted his big, hard muscled body pressing against mine. His big hard cock sinking into my wet, willing body. His soft lips nibbling on my neck. I kept thinking about it even though we'd both agreed it would be a bad idea.

Terrible.

But...would it?

I wasn't looking for love or marriage or any kind of long-term relationship. I wasn't even sure I'd ever want that at all. Ever. But I knew I didn't want it now. What I wanted though, was a long, hard fuck. And I wanted it from Tate.

But he'd made his position clear and I didn't chase after men, so I spent an extra half hour in the pool, cutting through the water to get rid of my sexual tension — or frustration. Between my sudden desire for Tate and this weirdo leaving creepy gifts at my house, I probably needed intense yoga and kickboxing. Every damn day.

By the time I got to the office, I felt cranky and pissed off, and in no mood to work. Of course, two minutes after I arrived, a very pissed off Kip Riley showed up. Without his camera crew. "What the fuck, Teddy?"

I glared up at him and stood to give myself a height advantage. "I should be asking you that, Kip."

He sucked in a deep breath and let it out as he sat on the other side of my desk. "The cops came to my house last night. Luckily Gillian had taken an Ambien or I'd be in some deep shit."

"Well you should have thought about that when you sent those creepy gifts to my house." I would never back down from these kinds of sleazy guys.

"I sent you flowers, Teddy. Sure, it was out of line considering you're planning my wedding, but flowers and chocolate don't warrant the friggin' cops." He huffed and raked a hand through his model perfect hair. "That's taking it a little far, don't you think?"

"You mean you didn't send the sliced up lingerie or the cleaver through my headshot, or any of that other creepy shit?"

He sat up, blue eyes wide with shock. "No. Fuck, I'd never do that. I'm trying to ride this reality gravy train until I'm a millionaire. I wouldn't fuck that up even for a hottie like you."

Shit. And I believed him. "Good to know, and I'm sorry. They asked and since you admitted you sent the flowers…shit. Just tell me you can prove it, because I'd hate to get an innocent man in trouble."

Kip grinned. "I just came from the police station with the footage of me nearly every hour of the day for the past six weeks."

My shoulders relaxed. "Good. But maybe wait until *after* the wedding to create the infidelity drama. And sign a prenup," I added with more than a hint of bitterness.

Kip laughed. "You're pretty cool when you take that stick out of your ass, you know."

"Yeah, I know, but I don't enjoy having cameras around all the time."

"Weird." He stared for a beat and then laughed. "You weren't always that way. I can still see you in that white Guess bikini," he said, closing his eyes and licking his lips like a lecherous teenage boy.

"Well back then it was my job. Now my job is to plan events." And I could admit I hated Kip a lot less now than I did when he and Gillian had walked into my office a few weeks ago. And then it occurred to me, it wasn't Kip but that didn't mean it couldn't be Gillian. "You should just stop all the flirting, though, to be safe."

He frowned. "Why?"

I couldn't tell him the truth, but one thing I learned in foster care and then modeling, is how to lie. "Because there will be hours of footage of you flirting and me pushing you away. If this becomes a thing, which it pretty much has, it won't matter that you're innocent."

It scared him just as I knew it would. Kip jumped up and smiled. "Thanks for being so cool, Teddy. I, uhm, hope this ends up okay for you."

"Thanks, Kip. See you and Gillian soon." He waved and left a trail of dust as he couldn't leave my office fast enough. One problem solved, too bad it wasn't the biggest problem on my plate.

The tone sounded above the door as a delivery man walked in, face hidden by the large bouquet that didn't make me as happy as he thought it would. "Delivery," he said with a bright smile I normally enjoyed.

"Thanks," I told him, though my words were half-hearted as he set the vase down on a nearby table. Black dahlias and black tulips with baby's breath, because we had to keep it classy, apparently. As soon as he was gone, I took the flowers to the dumpster out back and left them there.

This fucking day could not end soon enough.

***

"Oh my God, Jana, these ribs are so good. I hope you have leftovers." I licked my lips as I ate more ribs than a woman should, especially considering Max and Tate were looking at me like I was a science experiment. I didn't care though, not after Kip and the flowers, the useless cops and the sexual tension. Cannot forget the sexual fucking tension. Especially with Tate sitting beside me, his body emanating enough heat to melt the ice in my glass.

"Thanks, and yeah there are leftovers."

"No, there aren't," Max insisted with a frown, a bone sticking halfway out of his mouth. He flashed a smile at me. "Let's see where we are when the evening is over."

I laughed at Max, shaking my head at his foolishness. "I've been promised leftovers, Max. Deal with it. You get to eat this way every day."

He grunted and I couldn't tell if it was acceptance or refusal, but I knew Jana would hook me up. "There's already some set aside for you, Teddy."

"Damn, mama, I love you so hard right now."

She beamed a smile at me, probably feeling overwhelmed with emotions again, judging by the watery look in her eyes. "You're welcome." Her expression changed and I felt the hairs on the back of neck rise. "So, a meat cleaver, huh?"

I sucked in a breath and glared at Tate. "Seriously? You told her?"

He looked unapologetic as he crossed his arms and nodded, chin daring me to challenge him. "It was a damn meat cleaver, Teddy!"

"Yeah, I know. I recognized the face it cut right through," I told him, circling my face sarcastically. "Look, Jana, it's fine. I'm fine. At least I will be, if the cops do their job."

Tate turned to me. "What about that reality TV guy?"

I sighed. "They talked to him but he's been cleared, and he only sent the flowers."

"You can't go back there," Jana insisted.

"It's my home and I won't let some freaky-ass weirdo scare me away. I'll be fine, or I won't. Either way, you have more important things to worry about," I told her with a quick glance at her belly.

"Dammit, Teddy! I'm going to teach you some damn self-defense." Tate stood and grabbed my arm, "We can do it here or back at Max's place."

I looked up at him, hating that even at my height, the man towered over me. "Don't tell me what to do."

"My place it is," he said with a grin and tugged me out the door.

"Wait. I need my ribs, dammit!"

Max and Jana laughed, but my best friend didn't let me down, she brought me a plastic container filled with her delicious ribs and another with some potato salad. "There you go. Let Tate help you, please."

"Ugh, fine. Come on, *Golden Boy*, teach me to kill a man with my pinky." We stopped at my place so I could change, and thankfully, there were no gifts waiting for me. The drive to Max and Tate's house was mostly silent, except a few instances of me bitching about his high-handed ways. "Just because we're friends doesn't mean you can boss me around."

"I'm trying to make sure you can defend yourself," he said angrily and then scoffed. "Like that makes me such an asshole."

"Glad we're in agreement," I told him as we stepped from my car. He tried to get me to leave it at Jana's place, but I was too paranoid someone was following my car — or worse — tracking it.

He flipped me a smug grin. "You're a big ass ball of happy right now, aren't ya?"

I brushed past him to put my food in his fridge. I wasn't risking some asshole breaking in and poisoning it. "Yep. Come on, teacher. Teach me."

He rolled his eyes and removed his *kutte* and his long-sleeve shirt, leaving him in nothing but a very tight, and nearly see-through, t-shirt.

"Okay. Let's see what you can do."

He lunged forward and I kicked him in the balls, or I tried, but he deflected that quickly. Pretty damn quickly.

"Good try, but most men are prepared for that."

I nodded. "Okay. Again." All he did was lunge forward and I tried everything I could think of, first his face, which he avoided by a quick sideways move. Then his throat, his stomach and yes, his nuts. Again. Finally, in what I can only describe as a fit of annoyance, I stepped on his foot.

"Shit!" He lifted his foot, frowning even as his lips turned up into a grin. "Okay, well eventually something will work. But by then," he flipped me around so my back was flush against his front, "he could have a knife in you, several bullets, or just a tranquilizer to knock you out and take you wherever he wants."

"Crap!" His feet swept mine and a second later I was on the floor with his big body on top of me. Not a bad position in my opinion, but, "Cheap shot."

"This ain't UFC, Teddy. There are no rules. Fight dirty, do whatever you have to do to get free. And be smart about it." His breath smelled of beer and barbecue sauce, and dammit, I liked it. "See if you can get me off of you."

I bucked my hips against him a few times but the man was built like a goddamn tank. He wouldn't move until he was good and ready. I wiggled back and forth to no avail. My attempts at head-butting him only made him lean back. "I'm basically fuckin' dead, then." Which kind of sucked, considering how hard I'd worked to make something of myself. Twice.

"No, you're not. Be smart."

Is it wrong that I heard him say be a smart ass? I started to wiggle my body again, this time with more purpose. More focus on a central part of his body that slowly came to life behind his zipper. "Is that smart?"

He groaned. "Probably not smart of me to challenge you," he gritted out.

And just for shits and giggles, and because the man felt divine between my legs, I did it again. His breaths came faster, shallower than before as I wiggled. "Or it's the smartest thing you've done in a while," I said and wrapped my legs around his waist so he was pressed right where I throbbed. A moan slipped out.

"Teddy. Bad idea, remember?"

I nodded. "I do, but I've been thinking about it and it doesn't have to be. I'm not looking to be wifed up, Tate. I'm looking for a fucking orgasm. That's it." There was pause and I could tell he was thinking it over, considering it because I knew he wanted me as bad as I wanted him.

"You sure?"

I grinned. "See for yourself."

He rolled to my side, one hand propping up his head while the other slid easily into my workout pants and panties, finding me wet and slippery. "Fuck me," he groaned.

"That's the plan."

A deep chuckle sounded but two fingers slid into me the moment his mouth touched mine, pulling a moan from me. His fingers were thick and blunt as they slid deep, stretching me out. I didn't know where to focus, his delicious mouth, strong and firm, kissing me hungrily while his fingers brought me closer and closer to what I hoped would be my first orgasm of the night. "Fuck," he grunted as he broke the kiss.

"Yes," I moaned and gripped his shoulders, letting my hands roam freely over his big, hard body. He was all heat and muscles, all man. His fingers pumped harder into me and before I could slide my hand down to the bulge in his jeans, an orgasm ripped through me. "Fuck yeah…Tate!"

"Now that we've gotten that one out of the way," he began as he slid my pants and shoes off, staring at the wet spot on my panties, "I can take my time with you."

I sat up and removed my shirt. And bra. "Let's take our time later. Right now, let's go hard and fast." My hands were already at his waistband, tugging on the zipper when his hand stopped my own. "What?"

"It's been a while."

Oh right. Prison for six years. "Got it." I pushed him down on his back and undressed him like his clothes were on fire. But it was me, burning up with lust. My pussy dripped, pulsed and clenched with need for the hard prick that had been pressed against me. "You are a whole lot of man, Tate."

"Aww, you say the sweetest things."

"I do, don't I?" His words were cut off when I began kissing my way down his chest, partially for him but mostly for me. He was built with a capital 'B' and right now he was laid out like the perfect man buffet and I wasn't sure where to start first, those bulging tattooed biceps, the pecs with the dark pink nipples or my personal favorite, the rock hard abs I knew would be slightly salty from his sweat. In the end, I was a greedy bitch and tasted every inch as I made my way to the hard cock cradled between my breasts.

I looked up at Tate who watched with gray-blue eyes, teasing him with my smile. I didn't take him in my hand, not right away, instead I crouched down and licked him from the underside of his sac to the slit at the tip of his cock.

"Oh, fuck," he said on a long, guttural groan. I did it again and again, finally taking him in my mouth when his hips began to buck against me. "Fuck," he said, over and over as I sucked his big cock, swirling my tongue around it and using my lips to create more friction. He tasted good and his cock was perfect, long and thick and straight. My pussy grew wetter just anticipating having all that man meat thrusting inside my body.

"Teddy," he warned, but he didn't need to, I felt his cock harden and I felt his come working its way out under my fingers and I sucked even harder as that first salty drop hit my tongue. I sucked it all down while he grunted and thrust up, going deep and turning me on.

I moaned when he grabbed a handful of my hair, slowly sliding in and out of my mouth as he worked out the last of his orgasm. When his body went limp, I licked the last little drop and grinned. "Now I think we can go hard and fast."

He chuckled. "Thanks for the vote of confidence, but I'm gonna need a few minutes to recover."

I grinned. "That's okay because I have an idea how we can speed it along."

"Oh yeah?"

I nodded and kissed my way up his body, damn near sitting on his chest. "I want to grab all this hair while I ride your face. Hard and fast. Cool?"

He growled and smacked my ass. "More than. Come on, Cover Girl, don't be shy."

Even if I was shy, which I wasn't, I was too turned on, too eager to test his oral skills to worry about it. I slid into position and looked down with a smile. "Make me scream, Golden Boy."

Chapter 9

Tate

Hearing her say those words to me, *make me scream,* unleashed something primal, something animal in me. It was something more powerful than I'd ever felt because I knew Teddy wasn't just saying it to make my dick hard or because she wanted anything other than pleasure. That just made me want to make her scream twice as loud. "Challenge accepted," I told her, keeping my eyes trained on her as I slid my tongue deep inside her wet cunt.

"Oh, fuck!" Her hips began to move in an up and down motion, riding my face just like she wanted. Back and forth she went and I kept my tongue flat so every drop of her burst onto my tongue and slid down my throat. "Yes," she screamed when I sucked her clit into my mouth. She smiled down at me, grabbing my head so she could see my eyes as she rode my face. "Oh, Tate, fuck! Yes!"

She was close and my cock was hard again, ready to pound into her dripping pussy. "I can't hear you."

She looked down with a mischievous glint in her eyes as she rode harder. Faster. Her voice trembled through her screams when I grabbed her ass to help her move faster and her hands moved from my head to the floor as her hips moved lightning quick. "Oh, fuu-uuck Tate!" She cried my name, squealing as she rode out her orgasm, fast and then slow while I drank her. Ate up her juicy pussy.

I pulled her clit between my teeth and sucked it one last time, sending her body into quaking aftershocks that made her laugh. "Maybe I should call you *Cowgirl* instead of Cover Girl."

She laughed as she slid down my body and laid one hell of a kiss on me, licking hungrily at the taste of her all over my face. "Fuck. After that, you can call me whatever you want."

I gripped her ass cheeks, kneading them in my hand. She was so soft and pliant, and the way she relaxed under my grip, her juices coated my cock.

"Even Cover Girl?" She pretended to hate the nickname but her lips always curled up just a little in amusement.

Her hips rolled, dragging her sweet wet pussy up and down my prick and I grew harder, ached to slide deep and make her scream my name. "Even that," she said and tossed her head back, so her red waves cascaded down her back. Hands braced on my thighs, her hips rolled and dragged until I let out a low groan.

"Teddy."

She stopped and looked at me for a long, sobering minute and then she smiled and it was full of mischief. "Want something, Golden Boy?"

I nodded, spreading her ass with one hand and sliding a finger into her pussy from behind with the other. She let out a sexy little gasp and fell back on my hand. "Looks like I'm not the only one."

"Condom," she moaned.

In half a second, I was on my feet with Teddy in my arms as I marched down the hall and into my bedroom, lying on top of her as I laid us both on the bed. Max thought it was a big fucking joke when he'd given me that big box of condoms, but now I could kiss my brother. I pulled the box from the drawer and ripped it open, feeling her eyes on me.

"Uhm, big plans?"

I grinned. "Max thought it was the perfect gift for a guy straight out of prison. I wanted to kick his ass, but now I'm grateful," I told her, my gaze dark as she lazily circled two fingers around her pussy lips.

"Let me help you with that." She took the condom and tore the plastic with her teeth. I was mesmerized just watching her, so sexy and capable and completely unashamed of her boldness. Long fingers plucked the latex disc from the package and she held it between her painted lips as she slid off the bed to stand in front of me. "Down you go," she laughed and pushed me back on the bed, leaning over me to slide the condom down my cock.

With her mouth. "Fuck, Teddy."

"Now you've got the right idea," she said and climbed on my lap, holding my cock with one hand as she impaled herself on me. "Oh fuck, I knew you'd feel like this."

I couldn't help but grin at her admission; apparently, I wasn't the only one who'd been thinking about it. After that though, all I could think about was the way she squeezed me tight in her body, the drag and pull against the nerve endings of my cock. I held her hips but let her lead until it became too much. Her slow, deliberate pace felt good but I'd been without a woman for far too fucking long. "Teddy."

Her response was to move faster and faster, circling her hips as her pussy began to pulse. Leaning forward, she kissed me and began to ride me hard and fast, slamming down onto my cock with enough force to break both of us in two and I couldn't look away from her bouncing tits, mouthwatering pink nipples begging to be tasted. Sucked. Licked.

"Fuck, Tate. Yeah!"

I couldn't take it anymore. "Teddy, I need to fuck you." Before she could answer I flipped our positions and gripped her thighs, spreading her wide so that pretty pink pussy smiled up at me and I thrust deep, fucking her like my life depended on it.

"Fuck me, Tate. Hard and good. And deep."

I growled and gave her just what she asked for, sliding my dick deep until she clenched around me before pulling it out, coated with her juices. I gave her everything and took twice as much in return, pounding into her until my legs burned, my hips stung and my cock was so swollen and rigid my explosion was imminent. "Oh, fuck. Tight pussy."

"Wet pussy, too," she purred as her hand made its way to her clit, rubbing circles furiously.

Ah, fuck, watching Teddy play with her clit while my cock sank in and out of her, thrusted, pounded hard and deep, was enough to snap my control. I pulled her closer to the edge of the bed, wrapping her long legs around my waist, slamming so hard that the sound of slapping, slick skin mingled with her cries and my grunts. She wrapped those long, perfectly manicured fingers around my arms and let go.

It was the hottest shit I'd seen in at least six years. Maybe forever. "Oh fuck, Tate. Yes, yeah, oh yeah. Tate!" And then she was falling apart, pussy tightening all around me as her juices made the path even smoother. Slicker. "Fuck," she cried as one last rush of orgasm ripped through her, milking my cock to the sweet sound of her sexy cries.

"Fuck, babe." I pounded harder and faster until I felt my balls grow tight, my spine tingled with anticipation and then Teddy's name escaped on a roar as I emptied into her still convulsing body. "Shit, Teddy."

Her breaths came fast and shallow, nipples hard as diamonds and skin pebbled with goose bumps; she looked like some kind of sex goddess. "Damn Tate, that was better than I thought it would be."

I couldn't help but laugh at her plainly spoken words. "Didn't you know…I'm a master?"

She bit her lip on a moan when I slid free of her body. "I'm gonna let that slide because you dick-matized me."

I froze. "I did *what?*"

She sat up on her elbows, tits high and perky with still-hard strawberry nipples. "You left me dick-matized, Golden Boy. As in the dick was so good I can't think of anything else."

I laughed long and hard at that, even while I cleaned up and disposed of the condom. Dick-matized. I'd never heard that shit before...but I liked it. "For that one, I'll let you rest before the next round starts."

Blue eyes rounded in surprise as her eyes slid down to my still half-hard cock, and she licked her lips. "Next round? You mean there's more?"

I nodded. "Then self-defense."

She pouted. "Self-defense," she groaned. "Definitely after round three."

I slid beside her on the bed and pulled her close until my cock nestled between her tight, round ass. One hand caressed her breast and she was already squirming against me, making my cock hard again.

This chick was going to kill me, and I was damn well gonna let her.

***

"Damn, Golden Boy, who knew you'd be the kind of boss to order lunch for us?" Dallas smiled up at me as he looked inside the box of food that had just been delivered to the shop.

"Lasso, what the fuck, man? I didn't order shit." But the guy had said the meal had been paid for and his tip was included, too. "Hey," I called to the delivery kid before he made it out of the shop. "Who paid for this?"

"Oh shit!" He grinned and turned back, digging something out of his pocket, a blue sticky note, and shoved it at me. "She said to make sure you read this before you, uhm, dig in. Hot chick, too." He made sure I saw his good-natured grin as he walked away.

"Read it," Lasso urged. "I need to know if I'm gonna be poisoned when I tear into this."

Fucking guy was as big as three men with an appetite as huge as his home state. I unfolded the note, feeling a lot like a high school kid trying to open a note from a girl you liked on the down low so your boys didn't notice. But as soon as I read it, I barked out a laugh.

Since you ate my taco so well. T

That was it and I fucking lost it, doubled over laughing in the middle of my shop.

"Man, now I gotta read it," Lasso said, stalking over to me trying to snatch it out of my hand.

But I sidestepped in time. "Back up asshole. Eat the food but leave the note alone."

He shrugged and opened up one of the bags with a wide grin. "Fuck yeah, tacos!" He finished one taco in two bites, moaning like a fool and all I could think of was how fucking sexy Teddy sounded when she rode my face. "I don't know who sent them or why, but I fucking approve, boss."

I rolled my eyes. "Well guys, if Lasso approves, that's what matters."

"Damn right," he said with his big boyish grin. "Shit, there's guacamole too. Whatever you did, keep it up, bro!"

Jag strolled over looking like he'd just got done fucking. His deceptively lazy gait hid one of the sharpest minds I'd ever come across. "And they are fish tacos," he said and grabbed three. "What do you want, boss?"

I glared at him. "Just make sure you fuckers leave me something to eat. I got a few piercings coming in any minute." I sounded like an asshole I knew, and I couldn't help it. Hell, I didn't even know why. The tacos were a nice gesture and the note was just so Teddy. The bell sounded over the door and I held back a groan when I got the two young girls I assumed were my next appointments. "Grace and Amanda?"

Two sets of cheeks turned hot pink as they both nodded. "Yep," the brunette said, trying her best not to look intimidated.

"It's okay sweetheart, we won't hurt ya," Lasso told her and the girl practically fainted under the power of his Texas charm. A pause and then he added with a wicked grin, "Well, I guess that depends on whatcha getting' pierced."

"M-M-My tongue and we're both getting belly button rings." The blonde flicked her hair over her shoulder expertly and pushed her chest out toward Lasso. "You work here?"

His grin widened but I could see the little shit starter's eyes gleaming with funny business. "I do. How old are you?"

"I'm nineteen and Grace will be twenty tomorrow," she said, pointing to the brunette whose green eyes were still bugged out. "Why?"

"Because I was trying to decide if you were worth pushing back my lunch," he told her as his gaze swept over her tiny Daisy Duke shorts and a pink tank top that stopped at her ribcage. He glanced over at me. "You mind, boss?"

"Not at all," I told him. Better Lasso find the kind of trouble teenage girls brought with them than me. "What about you, Grace. You want Dallas here to pierce you too?"

"Okay," she squeaked out and took a step closer to her friend.

"Jag, take care of the paperwork and then have lunch. Lasso, be good."

"I'm always good." He patted his broad chest and drew both sets of female eyes toward his linebacker physique. "And I'm much better at soothing skittish girls than you."

That much was true. I headed to the back to restock a few things we'd gone through over the past week. Luckily business was good so I didn't spend all damn day and night doing shit like receipts and inventory. Right now, though, this was exactly what I needed to keep my mind off of Teddy and her hot little body, long legs and those sexy fucking noises she made in bed. It'd been a full week since we'd fucked, and still I couldn't stop thinking about it— or her. She was bold and sexy, confident and all about pleasure.

That shit was fucking intoxicating.

"Boss you got a customer," Jag called out, but there was something off about his tone. It was amused, but not, and that meant one thing.

"Sheena," I barked when I saw her. "This area back here is for employees and you don't work here. Go wait up front."

She stomped her foot and pouted. "Reckless Bitches—"

"Don't work for me." I wouldn't be nice about this shit anymore. "Are you here for a reason?"

Her whole body relaxed, softened as she stepped forward. I took a step back and held my hands out in front of me. "I was hoping we could both...*come*."

"Jag, get her out of here please. And if you see her in here again, remove her again."

"Sure thing, boss." Jag wiped his hands on a napkin and stood. With dark brown skin and twenty-inch biceps, Jag cut an imposing figure to anyone with half a brain. The man was harmless, unless he was forced to be deadly.

"No need for that shit," she snapped, glaring at Jag. "Touch me and I'll call the cops," she sneered.

"Excellent idea. Jag, can you report we have a trespasser on the property?"

"Golden Boy," she whined and stomped her foot again. "We could be so good together. I'll let you fuck me any way you want me."

"Not. Interested. Are you here to get a tattoo or a piercing, Sheena?" I knew the answer was no but she knew it was the only way she could stay and I could see the minute she decided.

Her hair swished around her shoulders when she nodded. "I want another navel ring. Two of 'em will be real sexy, don't you think?"

I shot a look at Jag, who'd gone back to enjoying his tacos while the sounds of Lasso entertaining the teenyboppers filled the front of the store. "When you're done with lunch, can you handle this?"

Jag nodded, trying hard not to smile. Everyone loved Jag. He was funny and nice, smart as fuck and got along with everyone. Except Sheena. She treated him like the white trash racist she was, but the truth was, she'd tried to fuck him and he wasn't interested.

"I don't want *him* to do it! I'm the customer and I want you to do it." Arms crossed, she gave a satisfied smile as though that fucking settled it.

"Well you see, Sheena. It's my shop and I reserve the right to refuse service to whoever I want. So Jag will do it, or you can leave. Now." A quick glance at the clock in the tiny closet that passed for our break room and I knew my next appointment would be arriving soon.

Hurt flashed in her eyes but, the hard woman that she was, she replaced it with anger. "You're not such big shit, you know, Golden Boy? You've been in prison for a long time and I don't see any bitches knocking down your door."

I laughed. "Don't you worry about my door, Sheena. My door, my life, my bitches are none of your fucking business."

Movement sounded in the break room as Jag finished and washed up before stopping beside me. "Are we doing this piercing or are you leaving?"

That was Jag, no-nonsense to his core. It would piss off a hothead like Sheena, but he was the kind of man you wanted on your side when shit went down.

"Ugh, come on then, I don't got all day."

"You mean you don't *have* all day," Jag corrected, chuckling when she let loose a string of impressive curses.

The bell sounded above the door and moments later, Lasso yelled out, "Boss!"

Sheena growled and Jag swore under his breath as Teddy walked in, looking hotter than fuck in an orange-ish pink tank that cupped her delicious tits perfectly, but her long legs were hidden by a long, flowing skirt the same color as her top but with big ass white flowers. "Teddy."

"Tate," she said smoothly, lips pursed slightly but when she slid those designer shades away from her eyes, they were lit with humor. "You ready for me?"

"Fucking slut!" Sheena's shout brought all the noise in the shop to a screeching halt. "I thought I told you to stay away."

Teddy arched one auburn brow and shot back a bored look. "And I thought I told you to take that up with whoever would be dumb enough to catch a case of the herp from you." She flashed a sweet smile up at me and then Jag. "You must be Jeremiah."

"Jag, ma'am. What gave it away?"

She grinned. "Well the cowboy is over there turning two sweet girls to mush so you must be the organized one."

"Not the black one?"

She laughed. "Obviously you're black, but all I heard from chatty Cathy over here was that one of you was a cowboy and the other one was the logistical genius."

"Genius, eh?" Jag smiled over at me and I punched him in the shoulder.

"Are you coming, Jag? I ain't got all fucking day." Arms crossed, Sheena tapped her foot to make sure everyone knew how unhappy she was. "Make sure you watch yourself bitch, it'd be a shame if something happened to that other leg."

I stepped forward, ready to deal with Sheena but I didn't need to. Teddy stepped closer to her, towering over the woman by at least five inches. "You better bring a fucking car because it's the only way you'll get me. Now run along before I get mean."

"Damn, I want to be her," one of Lasso's girls whispered.

Teddy's lips twitched as she stared at me and I swear, as cheesy as that shit sounded, I was caught in her blue gaze. "So, where do you want me?"

I took a long moment to appreciate the beauty that was Teddy Quinton. She was long and lean, but now her arms were sculpted and I knew her abs and legs were too. She was effortlessly beautiful and when she tried, she was goddamn stunning. "Sorry to tell you, Cover Girl, but I think you're wearing the wrong clothes for this job."

She laughed as I guided her to the first room past the register and slid onto the red leather seat. "First of all, there's no such thing as the wrong clothes. Unless of course it's acid wash," she added a little louder than necessary. "Second of all," she said and grabbed one side of her skirt and pulled it back, revealing one-mile-long leg. Her head fell back when I cupped her calf and let my hand slide up her leg. "You can work with this?"

I shrugged. "As long as you don't mind having your skirt open like that for the next few hours."

"Not like you haven't seen it all before. Anyway, I do have on panties so there's not much to see."

Lasso chose that moment to duck his head between the curtains. "Did someone say panties? Well hello, gorgeous. Is this the taco lady?"

She laughed. "I hope that's not what I'm being called, cowboy."

He blinked and his smile widened. All I could do was shake my head at the relentless flirt. "Who said I was a cowboy?"

"Besides those jeans?" she asked, drawing a loud guffaw from the Texan.

"I like her," he said with his best boyish grin. "If you get tired of the pretty boy over here, the name's Dallas."

She laughed. "Have you seen yourself? Your face is as pretty as his hair," she said and ran her long manicured fingers through my hair until I groaned.

Lasso's grin faded. "That's my cue to leave. Going to eat some tacos, boss."

"Listen for the door," I told him and pulled the curtains shut. Then I turned to Teddy. "Ready?"

She nodded but I could see the nerves in her blue eyes. "As ready as I can be, I suppose. Be gentle."

"Always."

Chapter 10

Teddy

One week. Those two words acted as my mantra all day because, for some reason, my focus was shot. Last minute wedding planning for Kip and Gillian, plus another new couple who wanted a midnight Elvis wedding in two weeks wasn't a lot for me. Yet, as I left the office with several assistants still making calls and picking up items for this weekend's wedding, all I wanted to do was go home and pass out.

I was searching in my tote for my car key and I heard, "Teddy! Teddy, we need to talk." Gillian Frye was tottering up the sidewalk in stilettos she could barely walk in, wearing skintight jeans and an adorable pink crop top that made her look at least a decade younger than her twenty-five years.

"What about, Gillian?" Though based on the scowl she wore and the way her hands fisted at her hips, I could guess.

"Kip. I know you're sleeping with him and I want you to stop." I opened my mouth to tell the fool how wrong she was, but a hot pink nail pointed at me before I could. "I don't care that you used to be somebody or that you're still hot, I want it to end or I will end you."

I could've eviscerated her with just one sentence, but that would be like kicking a newborn puppy. So, I decided to be mature. "First of all, I don't sleep with other women's men. Period. It's too much drama and I've yet to meet a man worth it. Second, you need to talk to Kip. He's been hitting on me for weeks and I shot him down. I don't fuck around with pretty boys."

She sucked in a breath, skin flushed an ugly shade of red. "I don't believe you."

"And I don't care, but it's the truth. Look Gillian, you seem like a nice girl so I'm going to give you some advice. Kip is young and newly rich and if you really want this to work, not just for the cameras but for real, you need to speak up. Men need to be handled so if you're not happy with his behavior, let him know. I don't want him, believe me, but one of these women out here will and they'll have no problem with the fact that someone else is wearing his ring."

It was more than I wanted to say, but she seemed like a girl out of her depth with the Hollywood game. If she didn't toughen up, she'd end up being one of those sad reality starlet stories.

"I followed him, Teddy. I saw him come here early in the morning. Without any cameras, and Kip will barely take a shit without a crew in the house. I believe you, but I also believe what I see." She pointed from her eyes to mine for emphasis and I shook my head in disbelief. Shit. Could she really be as naïve as she looked?

"I'll tell you, Gillian. But if I hear one word of this on your show or in any kind of press, I'll use my money and whatever star power I have left to ruin you both. Got it?"

Green eyes went wide with shock, she nodded quickly and a long ponytail bobbed behind her. "I swear."

I took a deep breath and let it out. "Someone has been leaving, let's call them *gifts*, outside my house. The first time it was Kip, so when the others appeared, I assumed it was him. Incorrectly, it turns out, but the police showed up at your house and he got scared. Worried and wanted to talk without the cameras. That's it."

"Oh my god, Teddy! Are you all right?" Her eyes were even bigger now, like the queen's emeralds, and I really hoped she didn't get chewed up and spit out in this industry. "I'm so sorry this is happening to you."

"Yeah, me too. But whoever it is doesn't seem to be targeting my office, so your wedding will go off without a hitch. I promise." She opened her mouth to protest and I held up a hand to stop her. "No, Gillian. Don't worry about this or me. Just pamper yourself so you're beautiful and blissed out on your wedding day. I'll take care of the rest."

How I ended up comforting her, I had no clue. But it was all part of the job.

"Thank you again, Teddy. And I'm sorry for the accusations."

I grinned. "I respect you more for coming to me. Just keep that shit up, okay?"

She nodded, squeezed me in a hug I didn't ask for but accepted, because I wasn't a complete asshole, and tottered back off to her sleek little sports car. She'd come without her entourage, which was a testament to how worried she was about Kip and how genuine her feelings were for him.

With that distraction out of the way, I jumped into my car and put on some NWA to clear my mind on the drive home. Between that knockout sex with Tate, which I still wasn't ready to even think about, let alone talk about, and the stress of this stalker, gangsta rap was the only thing that could help me. And I didn't give a damn who watched me rap along, complete with hand gestures, because that was just how bad I needed to lose myself in the music.

My love of rap music was the only thing that had followed me from foster care to fashion and all the way out to Vegas. By the time I pulled into my driveway, I felt about ten percent more relaxed than when I left the office, and considering the past few weeks, that was a win.

Until I got to my door and saw a sight that finally had me worried. The last two gifts had taken on a different tone than the first six or so. The photo was a clear threat, but what faced me now, as I dialed 911, was as overt as a threat could get. A giant blue dildo with a knife through the center hung on my door, both of them on top of a photo, I assumed of me. "Die Bitch" was written in red paint on my door but it looked like the blood it was meant to resemble.

I did as the 911 operator instructed and went to sit in my car while I waited for the police. A tap on the window startled me and I realized I should've been paying better attention. Just because this weirdo hadn't shown his face yet, didn't mean he wouldn't.

I smiled. "Mrs. Welliver, how are you?"

She wore a frown, but I could see her concern and I stepped out of the car to talk to my neighbor.

"Honey, I'm worried. What's going on?"

"I wish I knew. Someone, it seems, doesn't like me all that much." Not that it was a surprise, I didn't do much to endear myself to anyone but my clients, but this was something else. "You should probably get back inside before the police come."

She was at least seventy years old, but as active as a woman half her age. Still, I didn't want her caught up in this.

"I'm packing, sweetheart, don't you worry about me," she lifted her denim jacket to show the handle of a gun.

"I want to be like you when I grow up, Mrs. Welliver."

She winked. "I'll go have a seat in my rocking chair but send one of them over when they arrive. Make it a cute one too."

I was amazed that Mrs. Welliver could get me to smile after what I'd just seen, but the old woman was a character. And apparently a meddler because I turned around just as Jana slammed on her brakes and jumped from her car. She practically ran to me with Max following at a more reasonable pace behind her.

"Oh my god, Teddy! What's going on?" Jana flung her arms around me and squeezed tight and I looked at myself in the passenger window of my car, wondering if there was a sign on me that said I needed hugs. "Are you okay?"

"I'm fine Jana." I did my best to keep my voice even and calm. Didn't want to upset the pregnant lady. "I just got home from work and found it," I told her and pointed to the door. "911 said to stay here."

Max grabbed Jana's arm to stop her forward momentum and she glared at him. "They need to see if the asshole left any evidence, babe," he explained. "So they can catch him."

I had to give Max credit for daring to talk to Jana in such a reasonable tone when she was so wound up.

"Fine," she snapped, not sounding fine at all. "What is it?"

I sucked in a deep breath, closed my eyes and explained what I saw. "The knife through the dildo was jarring, but the 'die bitch' really got to me."

"This ain't funny," Max said in a low, lethal growl. "You'll come stay with us until this mess is settled."

I turned and glared at Max. It was my best glare, the one that could freeze a set of balls in less than three seconds, but Max was a bona fide badass and he didn't scare easily. "And put my pregnant best friend in harm's way? Yeah, I don't think so buddy."

I walked off before he could say more, heading off to greet the first uniformed officer who had just arrived. He asked questions and I answered them with more attitude than was necessary, but they hadn't taken me seriously at all over the past month. "I'm sorry ma'am, but we are taking it seriously now."

"Better late than before this psycho kills me," I muttered, forever a smartass. But when the forensic team finally arrived, dusting for fingerprints and bagging everything, I felt my knees buckle. It wasn't just a dildo-knife through a photo of me. It was a recent photo from a write up in Las Vegas Magazine, and my eyes were slashed out, my throat sliced from ear to ear and several holes in the Armani blazer I had on. To me, they looked like bullet holes, but the officer claimed they couldn't be sure yet.

Right.

"Can you think of anyone who would do this?"

Shaking my head, I shrugged. "No. I haven't been in the spotlight for years and I keep a pretty low profile. I'm not dating anyone and I work for myself. Honestly, officer, I am at a loss."

He nodded and walked away, and hours later when the sun finally set I was free to go. Where I would go would be a nice hotel suite with a big tub and kickass security.

Max and Jana still waited by my car. "I told you fools to go home hours ago. I appreciate you staying but one of you needs to rest."

"And what about you, Teddy?" Max's voice was angry and irritated. "Where will you go?"

"I appreciate your concern Max, but they have these things called hotels that let you stay there for a small fee each night. And they always have rooms available." Arms crossed, I gave him a defiant grin and waited for his response.

"Well that's all fine and well," began a familiar voice behind me. "But I have an available room and no fee."

I turned with a half-smile. "Thank you for the offer, Tate. But I'm going to have to pass."

He stepped closer and placed his hands on my shoulders. "I'm not asking."

"Good, then I won't feel bad about saying no." I stared at him, his gray eyes matching my blue ones in intensity, dogged determination and plain old stubbornness. I didn't want to give in, but I knew I would. Eventually.

His mouth curled up into a smile that sent me reeling. My body heated up and my skin tingled at the predatory look in his eyes. "Good. Then I won't feel bad for tossing you over my shoulder and carrying you."

Damn. I must be sick in the head, because just the thought of that is hot as fuck.

***

Nothing helps shove a trauma down deep like getting fucked within an inch of your life. At least, that was what I always said. And last night when I got back to Tate's, or Max's place — or whoever's house it was — Tate had been happy to oblige my need to forget. To just fuck for the sake of fucking.

And good Lord that man knew how to be a proper distraction.

The man groaned behind me, his grip on my stomach and my breast tightening. "You've been up for like one minute and already you're overthinking every damn thing."

I laughed at that. "How do you know I was even thinking, never mind overthinking? I could have simply been...*reliving*."

His teeth sank into the tendons between my neck and shoulder, his morning wood nudging insistently between my thighs. "Why relive in your mind when I'm right here?"

Why indeed? There was no need to answer him, not when he gripped my ass and spread my cheeks, slowly sinking into me from behind. I was drenched already, pulsing and aching for him as he slid slow and deep at first, but it was too good and my orgasm didn't seem to give a damn if Tate was close or not. He apparently got the message, gripping my hips tighter with one hand and pushing my back into a deeper arch as he pounded, hard and fast, and so damn deep it made me tremble. My legs began to shake and my breaths were shallow, hard to inhale as he slammed into me again and again.

"Oh, shit Tate! Yes! Fuck me...yes!" I should've felt ashamed of how loud and enthusiastic I was, but damn that was some good dick and if I wasn't careful, I might start jonesing for it. "Damn, that was better than coffee and vitamins in the morning."

His deep laugh sounded, turning into a groan when I joined in, the move making me clutch around his still hard cock. "Good morning to you too, Cover Girl."

I rolled my eyes at the name, but hell, I was used to it by now. "I should probably get up and check on my place." Though the thought of going back there made me sick to my stomach. Even though feel-good sex hormones still coursed through my body, the image came back to me quickly. Someone really wanted to fuck me up and I released a long, shuddery breath at the thought.

"No, you're not."

"I am too, dammit." I pushed off the bed but he grabbed me around the waist. "Let me go!"

"Just stop!" His words stopped me. I was ashamed as hell to admit it. "Max said they were planning on processing everything since there were some, uhm, things inside. Long story short, your place is off limits for a few days."

"No! Goddammit, this isn't happening." His grip loosened, and I took the opening to get out of the damn bed and put some distance between us.

"I know Teddy, it's shit. But there's nothing we can do about it today. Now get your pretty little ass in the shower because I have a meeting at the club in an hour."

I whirled around, not giving a damn about my nudity, though the look in his eyes as he took me in had me close to agreeing to do just about anything. Including hanging out at biker gang headquarters. "I don't need to go with you, you're a big boy Tate." Very big.

He smirked like he could read my thoughts. "I'm in charge of keeping you safe, which means for the time being, you go where I go."

His damn jaw was set in that determined clench that looked like it could crack marble and my shoulders fell. "Fine, whatever." He chuckled as I marched away, laughing out right when I slammed the bathroom door behind me.

"Save me some hot water," he called out, his voice still ringing with amusement.

With an evil smile I stepped into the mint green tub and turned on the shower spray before I called out, "Sorry, can't hear you!" Being around Tate was fun and waking up with a big strong body wrapped around me was a new experience because I never stayed the night with a man. Sex was one thing—trust was something entirely different.

But, I had to trust Tate, at least for today, so I kept my comments to myself as we entered the converted airplane hangar he called their clubhouse. "Doesn't look very clubby," I told him. "Looks like a bar designed by boys. Boys with questionable taste, at that."

"It serves its purpose," he grunted back, fixing a fake ass smile on his handsome face. "You'll be okay for a little while?"

I patted my laptop bag and nodded. "There's always work to be done. Just show me where I can charge if I need to and give me the Wi-Fi info and I'm good."

He flashed a bemused smirk and guided me to one of the small metal bistro tables near an outlet. It was far enough from the pre-party atmosphere so I could work undisturbed and that was good enough for me.

"Try and stay out of trouble, Cover Girl."

"I make no promises, Golden Boy." I watched his ass, snug in worn denim as he walked away. Tate was one fine man, and the fact that he stood up to help me, meant he was also a good man. I'd met so few of those in my life, it'd taken me until this moment to realize it.

But I had work to do. Fleshing out the final details for the upcoming wedding this weekend and making sure that everyone had the final schedule. With a big ass camera crew stomping around everywhere, I needed everyone to arrive at least thirty minutes earlier than scheduled and send out individual and mass emails to get my point across.

With that done, I turned to my file on Jana and Max's wedding. Between the two of us, Tate and I had gotten a lot of information from the lovebirds and I decided on a surprise engagement party at the clubhouse. But before I could set a date, I made a note to talk to Tate.

"Hey beautiful, why are you over here all by yourself?" The voice was gruff and when I looked up, my eyes met a pair of sea green ones lit with charm and sex appeal. And youth, because he couldn't have been more than twenty years old.

"Working while I wait for Tate."

Shoulders slumped, he shook his head. "Damn, Golden Boy still has all the luck with the ladies. I'm Zig," he said and held a hand out to me.

"Teddy," I told him and took it, appreciating his strong handshake free of any smarminess. "Nice to meet you, Zig. What's your role here?"

"A little of this and that. Mostly agriculture."

"Interesting. Did you grow up on a farm?"

"Ohio," he said with a mile-wide grin and held his arms out wide, showing off a wide chest and ripped arms filled with tattoos. "Born and raised. Though this gig is much better than mucking out stalls and stepping in pig shit."

I laughed at that, appreciating his candor. "Much better product too?"

"Definitely. If you need anything Teddy, I'm on the bar for another few hours."

"Thanks, Zig." He was nice, just like the guys who worked the tattoo shop with Tate. Sure they were all big as shit, with big muscles and bodies covered in tattoos. The leather vests stating their identity only added to the badass persona they perpetrated, but so far, they were all nice guys.

Charming, even.

But the women who draped themselves over tables, men playing cards and even the pool table at the center of the room. They wore pretty much the same outfit, same kind of skintight denim, black shoes and skimpy tops that showed off tons of cleavage, midriffs and plenty of tattooed arms. And each and every one of them had a dirty look for me, like I was some kind of threat.

That was fine with me. Women always treated me like I was some tramp out to steal their men, and nothing I said or did ever changed their minds. So I didn't even try. I stood and stretched my stiff back before stepping outside. Head tilted toward the sun, a smile crept over my face, a genuine smile despite the shit show my life had become.

"Now that's a smile I'd kill to have."

I jumped at the voice, so close to me, yet I hadn't even noticed anyone. That kind of awareness would do nothing to keep me alive. I turned at the sound of the voice to see a petite woman with hair so blonde it was practically white and cut in the most adorable pixie style. She had big green eyes that made her look like an anime character. "You can have the smile, it was as phony as a two dollar bill."

She laughed. "Mandy. I'm just visiting, not here to steal anyone's man."

I laughed at her words and her hands up gesture. "A woman after my own heart. I'm Teddy and I'm only here because my babysitter made me come."

She frowned. "So you're not a Reckless Bitch?"

"A what? I've been called reckless and I've been called a bitch, but I didn't realize there was a club."

Mandy shook her head. "No, it's what the club women are called. The ones who hang around and fuck the guys when they need it. They hook up hoping to become someone's old lady." She pulled a joint from her back pocket and sparked it up. "You look way too classy to be one of them. You have a kid with one?"

That pulled another laugh from me, a long hard laugh. "No. I've got a stalker. One of the guys inside," I thumbed over my shoulder. "Tate? His brother is engaged to my best friend, which means Tate got stuck babysitting me until shit blows over." I accepted the joint and took a long pull, letting the smoke filter through my veins until my body relaxed. "Thanks." I handed it back to her. "What are you doing here?"

She sighed as shadows fell over her face, and that haunted look I knew so well dominated her delicate features. "I just got back to town about six months ago and took a job over at Knead," she said, referring to the most coveted pastry shop in all of Vegas.

"Damn! I knew you looked familiar, but in the photo you looked more…mature. You're the hottest damn chef in the city!" I didn't fan girl over much, but Mandy was a big deal, and in my business, she was the holy fucking grail.

Her fair skin flushed prettily. "I will be, if I can keep my job."

"Well I'm always looking for a skilled pastry chef. Do you do wedding cakes?"

"It's been a few months, but in New York that was more than half of my work. Why?"

"I'm an event planner, mostly weddings, but this one is personal. I'd love a truly awesome wedding cake for my sister from another mister. Shit," I patted my pockets. "My bag is inside, but please don't leave without exchanging contact info."

"I won't," she promised and handed me the joint again. "Tate, isn't he the one who—" her eyes widened and I took a step back. "Sorry, but you're Teddy Q, the model, right? My god, I was so obsessed with you back in the day. Your long legs and that ass wore jeans perfectly. Shit, I loved and hated you for those legs."

"Well, they're still long but one is damn near useless," I told her.

She frowned. "What? They look fine to me, and I have to tell you that, yeah, right now I'm still kind of hating on your long legs."

I laughed, not bothering to fill her in on the missing pieces of the story. "I'm used to it, but that still doesn't tell me why you're here."

She rolled her eyes before answering. "Bossy. My brother was part of the club. He joined young because we needed money after our parents died. Anyway, he joined the military and...long story short, his friend Savior, that's who I'm here to see."

She seemed nervous and reluctant to talk and I respected her wishes. "I met him once, at the shooting range. Anyway, they're in a meeting right now and the women in there have turned staring into an art form."

"Thanks for the warning."

I shrugged, suddenly feeling way too relaxed to worry about anything that I should be, like work, an increasingly unstable stalker and my vandalized house. "Women always hate me," I blurted out.

"We treat each other worse than men ever could," she said, totally commiserating with me.

"Amen, sister."

The door pushed open, startling us both, but it was just Tate and his trademark smile. "I thought maybe you got antsy."

"I did, but someone stole my keys." I rolled my eyes and he laughed as he stepped out, the man they called Savior with him as both sets of eyes took in the blonde pixie.

"Mandy? Is that you?" The smile Savior had worn faltered, shifted into an uncomfortable glare. "What are you doing here?"

She flashed a shy smile. "I came to see you, Savior. I'd like to talk to you, if you have a minute."

He gave a sharp nod and held the door open. She ducked inside and he followed with a somber expression his face. "Damn that was tense. Oh crap," I remembered and ran inside, grabbing a card from my purse and pushing it into her hands. "Call me. Even if you just want to talk."

"Thanks."

"What was that about," Tate asked with a frown.

"Business and girl talk. We done here?"

His nod was terse, and he grabbed my elbow, standing guard while I packed up my belongings and we went back out into the sunny Nevada day. "Everything go okay?" he asked, a little more protective than earlier.

I looked over my shoulder with approval. "Aside from all the bitchy, evil looks, everything went fine. Actually, I was thinking we could—" my words were cut off by Mrs. Welliver's ring tone. "Mrs. Welliver, are you all right?"

"Honey, I'm sorry to tell you but someone set your house on fire."

I felt my knees buckle.

"I've already called 911, dear, but I thought you'd want to know. I'm so sorry," she said again.

"Thank you for letting me know, Mrs. Welliver. Stay safe, okay?"

"I will. See you soon, Teddy."

I disconnected the call and stared into space to get my thoughts together. Whoever this was, whatever they had against me, it was getting worse. They had gone from small gifts and threatening words to destroying my house. But I couldn't break down. I wouldn't.

"Is everything okay?" Tate asked, breaking my concentration.

"No. Let's go. Someone set the house on fire."

"Shit." He pulled my keys out, opened the passenger door so I could climb in, then he jogged around and jumped behind the wheel, burning rubber through the blacktop parking lot. He kept his foot on the gas until we turned onto my block to a sea of red and blue lights.

And my front yard and porch completely engulfed in flames.

Chapter 11

Tate

Teddy was shaken, she had to be given what we'd stood there watching for going on forty minutes, but to look at her, you'd never know. A close inspection would reveal tension around her eyes that were now blank, and her curiously straight mouth. Her shoulders were stiff as she stared at the flames licking up from the yard posing a mild threat to the rest of her small home.

She hadn't cried but she'd let out a mighty impressive string of expletives. "Fucking cocksucking motherfucker! When I find this piece of shit I'm nailing his balls to the table and setting the whole fucking thing on fire!"

I bit back a laugh, knowing she might test her torture out on me if I didn't. "Come on Teddy, we don't need to be here." I tried to pull her away, but she shrugged off my touch, turning to me with hell in her eyes.

"My house is burning down, Tate. I'm not going any goddamn where!"

I understood that but standing there and watching her use every ounce of energy and control to keep her emotions in check. And it made me feel damn helpless. I vowed never to feel helpless again so that made me fucking angry because I wanted to do something to help her. I needed to or the anger I worked so hard to keep to a simmer just might boil over and fuck up everything. "I know, Teddy. I'm sorry this happened."

"My house," she whimpered and I put my hands on her because I had to. One on her lower back and the other on her shoulder, to soothe her as much as me.

"It's fine, see?" I pointed to where three firefighters still gathered, dousing the last of the flames. No more orange and yellow in sight. Thank fuck. "Me and the guys can take care of that porch in a weekend. Maybe two."

She turned a shaky smile up at me, big blue eyes slick with unshed tears. "Thank you, Tate."

"None necessary, Cover Girl." I wanted to say more, but two plain-clothes officers headed our way. The same fucking detectives from before. Were there no other cops in this whole fucking town?

"Ms. Quinton, we have a few questions," the older detective, Haynes, said and then launched into a dozen questions I was pretty sure they already had the answers to. "Any more ideas on who'd want to hurt you?"

She shook her head, hands trembling. "I honestly have no idea and I wish I did, because this shit just got scary. Well, scarier," she added in an attempt at levity. Teddy ran a shaky hand through her long red hair to steady herself. The woman continued to impress me with her control.

"And you," the younger detective added with a sneer meant to let me know exactly what he thought about me.

"What about me?" I stood taller, using my height advantage to let him know I wasn't scared.

"Where were you when this happened?"

Teddy opened her mouth but I spoke over her. "Since I don't know when it happened and neither do you, I couldn't tell you. But I can tell you that I've been with Teddy since early this morning and had fuck all to do with this."

This fucker reminded me of the cops who put me in prison. They had their minds made up and nothing I said would change their fucking opinions.

"You sure about that?" He whipped out his small black notepad as if that shit was supposed to intimidate me.

"I don't need to be sure. You do." I stared at the rookie, so eager to look competent he didn't realize what an incompetent prick he seemed to both me and his partner.

"I'm watching you," he threatened.

I smiled. "You wouldn't be the first. Men hit on me all the time, but given the situation we find ourselves in, it's a tad inappropriate don't you think?"

That pissed him off good if that strange shade of pink his face had was any indication.

He screwed his face into what he probably thought was a tough guy sneer. "You little—"

But then his partner butted in. "Dodds, go talk to the woman who called it in. Take a detailed statement," he ordered, turning his back to the little fucker before he could voice a complaint. Haynes turned to me, his eyes shrewd but not suspicious. "You looking out for her?"

"Yeah, that's why she's with me until you figure out who's doing this."

"Any ideas?" He seemed to genuinely want to know but Teddy was drawing a blank.

"She used to be a pretty famous model, so it could be anyone, but—"

"That was a lifetime ago," Teddy cut in with ice in her voice, probably tired of the men talking about her like she wasn't there. She glared up at me and I smiled. "Detective, I wish I could give you some names but my life is boring. I hang out with my best friend who works from home, I keep my customers happy and I don't really date."

"Really?" He meant no disrespect, but a woman as beautiful as Teddy was expected to date nonstop, to use her beauty to land a rich and successful husband.

"Yes, really. And the guys I shoot down have no clue where I live."

"But they could find out. Anyone stick out as not being able to take no for answer?"

She let out a bitter laugh. "You know men, they all think 'no' is a starting off point in negotiations. If I'm not interested, I say so. If they don't get it, I say it clearer, so yeah, I've pissed off a few guys but I'm sure they found someone more willing to take home that night."

Shit. Was that what she dealt with when she went out? I couldn't even imagine having to deal with that and it pissed me off that *she* had to deal with it. "That's fucked up."

She laughed again. "That's called being a woman."

"Any angry girlfriends?"

"I don't fuck other people's men, detective."

Haynes held his hands up. "I meant no disrespect, Ms. Quinton."

She shook her head to brush off his apology. "If I did it was unknowingly, and it would've only been for a night, maybe two. And certainly not at my home."

His green eyes flashed but he quickly got it. "Thank you. I'll let you know what's going on, but you're free to go."

She nodded and turned to me as I wrapped my arm around her slender shoulders. "Thank you," she mumbled and I led her away.

"Come on Cover Girl, let's get you out of here." I planned to take her home and get her mind off this mess, at least until morning.

***

"I can't believe you chose tonight to work out the details of the engagement party." Shaking my head in disbelief at all the shit she'd laid out on the dining room table.

Teddy laughed. "Oh, come on, it wasn't that bad. Besides I needed a non-naked distraction for at least a few hours," she said but those blue eyes burned white hot as they landed on my mouth. Teddy had been insatiable over the past couple days, reaching out to me in her sleep, in the middle of a movie, or hell, even in the middle of dinner.

I knew what it was, too. Every time she got that faraway look and she wanted to banish it, she turned to me. And I didn't mind, not one damn bit, that a beautiful woman wanted me to make her forget some pretty awful shit. She did the same for me.

"It wasn't bad, just surprising. Whatever works, right?"

"Exactly. But now that we've got everything settled with the engagement party, maybe you can be what works?"

Her gaze darkened and she licked her lips, carefully setting aside lists, both handwritten and digital, and leaning her elbows on the table.

I nodded. "So you want to use me for my body?"

She nodded. "And your skills, but the good news is you can use me for my body."

And if that wasn't the kind of offer a man waited his whole life to hear, no one passed the message along to my cock because he was already twitching, hardening beneath the table. "And what a mighty fine body it is." Especially the way she looked right now, no makeup and her hair pulled into a sloppy ponytail. Fresh-faced and sexy as fuck.

"Bringing out the charm?" she asked as she stood and slowly walked around the table to straddle my lap. "I appreciate it. Besides," she licked up my neck and nibbled my ear, "you look really hot when you're charming."

I didn't know what to say but she didn't give me a chance, capturing my mouth in a scorching kiss that had me clawing at her back, squeezing her ass to get as much friction as we both wanted.

She drove me mad as she kissed me with a wild fever unlike any kiss we've shared, down my throat as her hands grabbed the hem of my t-shirt and pulled it up and off. Again, she licked her lips as she took in my body, even harder and more sculpted from six years of nonstop weight training.

"Like what you see, Cover Girl?"

She nodded, gaze darkening to damn near black. "Damn straight." Before I knew it, she was off my lap and on the floor between my thighs, tugging down my zipper to set my cock free. "This," she said with a breathless hunger that made my cock twitch. My hips lifted on their own and she pulled my pants down to my ankles, biting the tip of her tongue in anticipation before she licked my cock, over the head and up, down and all around my shaft.

"Teddy." Her name was ripped from my lips by pleasure, by the feel of her hot, wet mouth, the slide of her tongue licking from my sac to the head of my cock. "Fuck."

Her laughter vibrated through my dick, bringing me closer to the edge. She licked and sucked, taking me deep and pulling out until the cool air hit me and made my hips buck.

"Mmm," she moaned and I lost it.

"Oh fuck. Teddy!" She tugged on my balls and took me deep, so deep I could feel the back of her throat squeezing the tip of my cock. "Teddy," I warned again but she only moaned deeper and practically ate my cock as I came down her throat, my body jerked as her throat constricted around me. "Ah, fuck!"

I watched her head bob up and down, ponytail bouncing as she used her lips and tongue to bring me back to earth. "That's next." She stood and peeled off her shirt just as my phone rang and she froze. "Dammit."

With a laugh, I picked up my phone. "Yeah, what's up Max?" I listened to him talk, my hand roaming up and down the silky skin of her midsection, grazing a hard nipple. She gasped and my cock, still leaking, twitched. "Fine. We'll be there."

"No," she groaned. "I don't want to hear it."

"Jana is freaking out so we've been summoned for dinner." That was putting it mildly since Max's words were, *"Get the fuck over here and calm my girl down."*

"Oh shit!" Teddy grabbed her shirt and ran to the bedroom we'd been sharing since we first slept together. "I totally forgot to call her after the fire. She's probably freaking out." I found her in the bedroom shimmying into a pair of jeans and a bluish-green tunic that made her eyes pop. "Why are you just standing there? Let's get a move on."

With a smile I wiped off my cock and changed clothes. "Ready."

With a grunt she marched out of the house to the passenger side of her car, tossing me the keys. "And you so owe me when we get back tonight."

I turned over the engine and backed out of the driveway. "When we get back. You're mine."

"I'm holding you to that," she said, then blasted the radio and rapped along to some shit I'd never heard before.

By the time we pulled up to Max and Jana's, I'd gotten to hear her skills as a rapper. "Thanks for the concert."

She rolled her eyes, took a deep breath for strength, and slid from the car. At the door she was met with a very angry and emotional best friend. "Hey babe, looking good. And a little flushed."

I would've laughed if it didn't look like Jana might kill her. "Flushed? I drove by your house on the way back from the store, Teddy, and imagine my surprise to see your whole front yard and half your house black from fire. Fucking fire, Teddy!"

Teddy opened her mouth to protest, to explain or something. Whatever it was, Jana cut her off. "No. No excuses, Theodora! I was terrified that I lost you," she said, sniffling and exhibiting all the warning signs that tears were imminent. "Because that was the only reason I could think of why you didn't call me to tell me what had happened."

"Shit, Jana." Teddy wrapped her arms around Jana, looking a little bit guilty and a little bit weary. I was damned impressed by her, comforting someone else when just twenty-four hours ago she had been the one standing there traumatized, watching her house burn. "In my defense, I was a little shaken by watching my house go up in smoke so I went home and crashed. Besides you're pregnant and easily excitable."

"And?" she pulled back and asked indignantly.

"And your job is to keep that little peach safe, and I'm not letting my shit interfere with that. Deal with it." Her arms crossed and a defiant tilt of her chin dared her friend to say anything.

But Jana was emotional as hell, and clearly still upset by what she'd seen. "And how do you think I would feel if something happened to you?" She turned to me, green eyes flaring with accusations. "And you, Tate. Why didn't you fucking call me?"

I held my arms up and took a step back, right into Max. "I was more worried about her, honestly. She was kind of in shock after watching her house burn."

I would've apologized but Jana had sucked in a shocked breath and wrapped her arms even tighter around Teddy. "Shit, I'm sorry. That must have been terrible for you, Teddy!"

Max groaned and loudly clapped his hands. Right by my ears. "All right ladies, let's dry those tears and fill our bellies."

And just like that, the emotions had been diffused and we sat down to a fucking feast, but all I could think about was the feast I would have later. Between Teddy's long, silky legs.

Chapter 12

Teddy

"Thank you so much, Teddy! This day was perfect, just how I wanted." Gillian's eyes welled with tears that she kept expertly perched on the edge of her eyes, right where she wanted them. It was an impressive trick and I was sure it would look beautiful on camera. "This was...everything."

"I'm happy that everything was to your liking, Gillian. You're a gorgeous bride." She flushed prettily and ran off to join Kip, playing the role of besotted groom to a tee. Hell, he might actually love Gillian, I didn't know. And now that the wedding and reception were behind me, I didn't particularly give a damn, though I was sure cameras would follow them around during their first year of marriage. Not my circus, not my monkeys. The final check had been cut and the caterers were cleaning up while the camera crews broke down their lights and other equipment.

By the time I left the ballroom, the casino sounds were just obnoxiously loud and I picked up the pace as I headed out into the chilly night air. I couldn't stop yawning, but luckily the drive home would take less than twenty minutes with weekend traffic. But as I drew closer, I spotted a familiar figure leaning against my car. I smiled and yelled, "Hey! Get your ass off my car!"

Tate wore a mile-wide grin and pushed off the front, giving me a spectacular view of his ass while he walked around the car and pulled open the driver side door. "This ass goes where it wants. Mind if I drive?"

I slid over to the passenger side. When he was close enough, I gave those tight buns a squeeze and then I froze, looking around over my right shoulder and then my left. I had the feeling someone was watching me, but everywhere I looked revealed nothing. No faces or suspicious shadows. "Let's get out of here."

Tate frowned and raked a hand through his long hair. "What's up? Didn't tonight go well?"

"Oh, it went amazing," I told him as he put the car in gear. "It went fantastic and I was foolishly about to say how a few days had passed since the fire and there haven't been any incidents."

"And now?"

I looked to him and then my gaze darted to the side mirror. Still nothing. "Now, I just had a feeling someone was watching us." I knew it sounded crazy. I shook my head and let my gaze blur against the stop and go traffic.

"Hey, I believe you. I didn't see anyone but I know that feeling. It's saved my life a few times."

I wanted to ask more, but I hated thinking about the hell he lived in for six years. "I appreciate that, but I didn't see anyone. It was just a feeling." I'd hoped that maybe the silence over the past few days meant they'd scared me enough, but like Tate said, that feeling is there for a reason.

"I don't want to shit all over your good mood but usually these guys take a break before they escalate."

His white-knuckle grip on the wheel told me he hated saying it, but probably not as much as I hated hearing it.

"And you know this how?"

He shrugged. "I shared a cell with a man who stalked two ex-wives and an ex-girlfriend before he killed them all in the same night. He was able to do it by backing off for a few weeks, making them lower their defenses. When they did, he pounced."

That sounded terrible. "They couldn't have put you with someone normal? Just a serial killer?"

He barked out a laugh that surprised the hell out of me. He chuckled and smiled, but those bone-deep laughs were rare. And I loved the sound of them. "Since I wasn't a woman who'd rejected him, he was a pretty nice guy. I learned a lot about a lot of shit I never wanted to know about, though."

"Well," I laughed because this was the most ridiculous conversation I'd ever had. "I appreciate the lesson he passed on to you. Really." I looked around and realized we weren't headed to his house. "Where are we going?"

He quirked an eyebrow at me. "We're going to celebrate another successful event. Another week survived. And morning head," he said, teasing me about the treat I'd given him before he'd barely opened his eyes.

"So, we're celebrating the fact that you woke up with your dick in my mouth with a steak dinner?"

"I'm a simple man."

At that I had to laugh. "You are a lot of things, Golden Boy, but simple ain't one of them." He was complicated as they came, but not in a bad way. "You say what you mean and you show what you feel, but there's so much under the surface that you don't reveal. That, my friend, is the definition of complicated."

"Do you want steak or not?"

My lips twitched at how uncomfortable he was with the compliment. "Fuck yeah, I want steak — and lobster. But for dessert I think I'll have some man meat."

He laughed again as we walked inside the restaurant and I swore that sound shot straight to my core and soaked my panties.

***

"You know Teddy, it'll only take about an hour or two to finish this thing up." I could barely hear what the hell Tate was saying because his hand slid up and down my thigh in a slow, dragging motion. It could be the pot we smoked or the margaritas I'd made to go with the spicy beef tacos, but I was pretty sure it was just Tate.

Fucking Tate, who I didn't see coming. I was starting to have thoughts I shouldn't be having about any man, but especially Tate. Despite how great he was, how fucking fantastically hot he was, the man was practically family. When this thing, this hot sex we were having, ended, it would be awkward as fuck if one of us was dumb enough to catch feelings. "Fine, let's do it soon-ish."

"The hard part is done. Now it's just some shading and coloring the next time you come into the shop."

"Because it's just that simple? You forget, I've been through the other stuff and it hurt like a son of a bitch, Tate."

He chuckled, his hand grazing up and down my leg in lazy motions that shot straight to my pussy. "And that was the hard part. This will be nothing in comparison."

And he was so damn good. How a man who'd been wrongfully imprisoned could still be a good person was baffling to me. Most of the shitty people in my life hadn't spent one day in jail, and he was just good. And sweet. And hot. And, goddammit, I liked him.

"Hey, what's that frown for?"

And that was a problem I wasn't ready to deal with yet. So, I relied on my old standby. "Just thinking of the best method to seduce you right now."

He flashed that lazy, cocky grin, tugging my leg until one was draped across his lap. "These shorts are a damn good start."

Using his shoulders for leverage I pulled myself up to a sitting position, right in his lap. "I love this seat," I told him and ground against where he was already growing hard beneath his sweat pants. "It's so, ah, comfortable."

"You're wearing too many clothes," he bit out, eyes heavy and dark as I stood, shoving down my shorts and removing my tank top. Standing stark naked in front of the hottest man in all of Nevada, I felt my confidence swell. "Now that's the right amount," he practically growled and pulled me back on his lap.

Unable to resist, I cupped his face and kissed him hard and fast, hungry as fuck because the moment we touched my body became a greedy little slut, lapping up his taste, his substance like it was going out of style. Tonight, I couldn't get enough.

I wouldn't. "Fuck," I growled against his mouth as he slid a finger deep inside me, curving it at just the right angle to make me insane. "Tate." Head thrown back, I began to ride his hand, crying out when his lips wrapped around my nipple. Tugging hard just how I liked. "Yeah, like that!"

I felt my first orgasm pushing toward the surface and my hips moved faster and faster.

"You're so fucking wet. My hand is drenched."

"How about we get that cock nice and drenched?"

He let out a deep chuckle, using one hand to shove his pants down while he pushed me closer and closer to the edge. But I wanted more. I wanted his long, thick cock pounding into me. Hard, fast and rough. "Great idea."

His smile was irresistible and I had to taste it with my whole mouth. I kissed him again, hard and hungry as he gripped his cock and ran it through my wet folds. "Oh, fuck me."

"I intend to, Cover Girl." And then he lined our bodies up and I dropped down onto his cock with more force than necessary, burying him so deep it was damn near uncomfortable. "Oh fuck!"

He held my hips, but this was my show. Right there on the sofa, I rode his cock like the most award-winning rodeo girl on the planet. Stroking and grinding, I rode his cock hard and fast, greedy for him in a way I couldn't really understand. "Tate," I moaned as the orgasm rolled to my skin, ready to shoot through every pore like a supernova.

He gripped my hips and took over, yanking my hips in a frantic up and down motion that sent my senses reeling. He grunted and growled his pleasure and that ended up being what tipped me over the edge into a fracturing orgasm that tore me apart, left me shattered and shaking while he used my pulsing orgasm to reach for his own. "Ah, fuck Teddy," he grunted, hips still jerking up as emptied himself into my body.

I couldn't stop moving, even through the aftershocks, even though he was growing soft. I needed more of him. I was so goddamn hungry for him that I didn't stop until our bodies separated. "Damn Tate, that was incredible. Let's do it again."

He laughed. "Give me a few minutes." A moan escaped when he shoved two fingers to replace his much thicker cock. "Still clenching, dirty girl."

"It's not your beautiful cock, but I'll take it," I panted as I rode his hand to my second orgasm. Eyes locked together, he held me captive as my hips rolled hungrily against him, the small curve of his lips pushing me until I let go, screaming and shuddering around him.

"Speaking of beautiful," he said as I fell apart all around him, resting my face right over his heart.

In that moment, I knew Tate was going to be a whole different kind of trouble than I was used to.

Chapter 13

Tate

"And now your tattoo is officially, done."

I smiled down at my handiwork, proud of the rich colors and shadows on her long, sexy leg.

She smiled up at me and then down at her leg, standing and pulling her long skirt to the side. She looked at the ink in the mirror, her gaze riveted on what she considered her newly beautiful leg. "I love it, Tate. You did a great job!" That smile, the one I saw in my dreams, flashed wide and happy, and somewhere in the distance warning bells sounded. But dumb fuck that I was, I ignored them and smiled back.

"That's what I wanted to hear. That you love it." I pulled her back flush against me, gliding my hand up her ink free thigh as I kissed her neck. "I didn't think those legs could possibly get any sexier. Glad to see I was wrong." She shuddered under my touch, shivered as my warm breath tickled her neck.

"Yeah well, you have been without a woman for a long time." Deflection was something Teddy did a lot and always when it came to compliments, which was weird because she was as confident as they came. Except when it came to her scarred leg. "How much?"

I blinked, my lips still on the side of her neck, as her words sank in. "No charge. Consider it on the house."

She shook her head and stepped out of my arms. "No way, Tate. Don't be that guy, not right now." She peeled a few bills from her wallet while she sent very creative curse words my way. "Three fifty should be enough. If it's not, I expect you to let me know."

She was so fucking beautiful, standing there with her toned arms on display as she fisted her hands at her hips. Her blue eyes blazed angrily, red hair wild and unkempt.

"Stubborn damn woman," I muttered and reached for her, pulling her back into my arms so our bodies were pressed tight together. She was so soft and feminine, smooth and silky. I couldn't get enough of touching her, she was so responsive. I smacked her ass and lowered my mouth to hers, a scorching kiss that left us both wide-eyed and panting. Turned on again, just like that.

"It's one of my many charms, Golden Boy. I thought you knew."

"Oh, I know, baby. Let me wrap that up for you or you're going to get blood and ink everywhere. You need to keep it covered until tomorrow. And take some ibuprofen."

She held her skirt up while I wrapped plastic wrap lightly around her leg. My fingers grazed her panties in an attempt to make her squirm. And it did.

"Tate, my leg is on fire and you want to go there?"

"Nope. I'll let you heal. You like it?"

"I fucking love it! Thank you again." With that mischievous smile, she waved goodbye and pushed through the glass door.

"Damn man, you've got it bad!" Lasso laughed and clapped me on the back, ignoring the glare I sent his way. "Not that I blame you, Golden Boy, because that is a quality woman right there. Beautiful and strong, independent and sassy. Perfect for an old fucker like you."

I grunted a laugh at him, the way I always did when his Texas-isms got to be just a tad too country. "Glad you approve, Lasso. I can rest easily now."

His smile brightened. "Hey, no problem man. Glad I could help you see the light." The shop phone rang and I picked it up, still glaring at a laughing Lasso.

"GET INK'D, what can I help you with today?"

"Merry Mayhem, meet me there in twenty." Cross said what he needed to say and ended the call, leaving me staring at the phone like it might bite. "I have to go out for a bit guys, I'm being summoned."

Jag frowned. "Everything all right?"

I shrugged. "Hell if I know. He might want to chew me out just for being an asshole the past few weeks."

"Months," Lasso offered with a cough.

"Okay fine, months. Dick. Still." Shit was fine now. I did my part at the club and even employed a few of the guys. What the fuck else did they want from me?

"Maybe don't go in there wearing that face," Jag offered diplomatically.

"This is my fucking face."

Both of those fuckers laughed. "Try to look less like you want to rip someone in half, and more like you did when you were staring at your girl."

It was on my lips to deny that Teddy was my girl. She wasn't. We were thrown together by circumstances and mutual lust. "So you want me to ogle Cross? No thanks, he's not my type."

But I did take a ten-minute ride on my bike for a quick attitude adjustment. No good would come of showing up angry. I'd let Cross say what he needed to say, act appropriately, and then get back to work.

Merry Mayhem was near empty this time of day and I spotted Cross at one of the dartboards in back, a pitcher of beer on the table. He smiled as I got closer. "You came."

"You summoned me," I reminded him.

He frowned. "Is that how it is now? An invitation to hang out is now a summons?" His words were grave, sober and yeah, I kind of felt like shit.

"I'm starting to wonder now if you still want to be a Reckless Bastard." He looked at me, stroking several days' growth on his chin as he assessed me. I saw every damn emotion flash in his eyes. Anger, frustration and disappointment were the clearest to see.

"I'm here, ain't I? But that's not enough, is it? I show up to Church and do my part in club business, but it still isn't enough. What the fuck?"

Cross glared at me for a long moment before he turned to the board and fired out three darts, hitting two triple twenties and a bullseye. "This is us, Golden Boy. This club is our life, our family, our financial future. We do what we have to do to survive, we don't do this shit because we feel like we have to." He took an angry sip of his beer while I lined up my dart.

"It's not a goddamn obligation, Cross. But being around everyone has been hard since I got out the pen." I couldn't really explain why it was, just that I didn't feel as at ease with the club as I had in the past, and that shit pissed me off. Like Cross said, these guys were my brothers. My family. They had my back.

"That right there," he pointed at me at first angry and then resigned. "That look that you get, the one that sometimes says you're hatin' on us. What the fuck?"

"I don't know what you're talking about," I told him as I hit my third bullseye. "I don't hate you or anyone else. I love the club."

"You've been distant and I get that. Even though I've never served another man's time, I get it. But the anger toward us, I don't get that."

Yeah, well, I didn't get that shit either. "I don't know what to tell you, Cross. I'm doing the best I can."

"And that's why I wanted to come and have a drink with you. I see you're trying to get back into things, which means you want to be here. And I think I've figured it out."

"There's nothing to figure out, Cross."

He laughed and shook his head. "Savior said we should've talked to you about it at the time, but I disagreed. You know those calls at the prison aren't private unless you're with your attorney."

I gave a sharp nod. I knew it well. More than a couple inmates had been caught up with their own words. "Talk to me about what?"

"About the asshole who actually murdered Ricky Tran."

The fucker who'd died shortly after his DNA had been identified under Ricky's nails. With him dead though, the prosecutors had suppressed the information, or tried to because we'd gotten into a scuffle earlier that same night. "What about him? He's dead now, right?"

Cross nodded. "As soon as we got the ID on that DNA evidence we went after him, Alan Baker. No affiliation other than he fucking hated Asians. We made sure he understood the ramifications of not coming forward. He chose the alternative."

Both of my eyebrows rose. "A round with Savior?"

His face filled with evil happiness. "Jag. Figured if he hated people of color, he might appreciate the challenge. He did, but Jag did not." He shook his head, a wistful smile of remembrance on his face. "He didn't want to come forward. The asshole was more afraid of what would happen to him in prison than what we'd do to him. We proved him wrong."

I nodded at what he hadn't said explicitly and released three more darts, barely hitting the board. Singles all around.

"I'm telling you this so you know, Golden Boy. We had your back then and we have your back now. If I thought there was any chance of him coming forward to help, I would have dumped him in front of the cop shop myself. The fucker probably would have said you worked together, so we handled it. Our way."

I appreciated it. A lot it turned out. "Wow, man. I was ready to tell you to go fuck yourself, that I wasn't pissed at the club, but shit, maybe I was. Thanks for letting me know, Cross."

I didn't know what else to say because talking about my feelings wasn't something I did regularly—and definitely not with Cross. "You know, I am a Reckless Bastard down to my fucking bones. And I know I've been distant. But only because I needed to get my anger under control. If I hadn't fought with Tran that night, I wouldn't have ended up where I did for six fucking years."

"And that hot model you're dating is keeping you in bed whenever she can?" He laughed, his eyes lit with teasing as his brows waggled.

"She's a *former* model," I corrected and took a long pull of my beer, grateful the tension was gone. My body felt lighter, less weighted down now and I was able to smile. To finally relax. "And we're not dating."

We were fucking, plain and simple. Any and everywhere we could. Hard and fast, slow and tender, long and affectionate. Every goddamn night, too.

"It's okay if you like her," he said easily, his gaze searing into me to make sure I understood his words. "You deserve something good after what you've been through. I say enjoy it."

I was enjoying it. Too damn much, if you asked me. There was no way I could give Teddy anything a woman like that deserved in life. She'd had a shit run of things as a kid and then after, she deserved a man who would bring her flowers and do romantic shit. And we couldn't be more than what we were. "Yeah thanks, Cross. Want to curl my hair and paint my toes next?"

He laughed. "Nope. Just had a mani-pedi with Savior." He wiggled his fingers in my direction and we both laughed, finishing another round of beer in silence. Like men should do. But it was nice now that the distance was gone. It felt like old times.

Finally, I fucking felt like I'd left that prison for good.

Chapter 14

Teddy

The past few weeks had been relatively uneventful as far as my stalker was concerned, but that only made me worry more after Tate's less than helpful advice about stalker behavior. Every damn time I felt my body relax and the notion of safety began to sink in, all I could think of was that this was a trap. That the moment I let my guard down was the moment I'd end up dead like one of Tate's cellmate's victims.

So, I stayed inside. With the exception of work, I rarely left the house anymore because my nerves were such a twisted jumble of anxiety. Even something as simple as going to Jana's house filled my mind with images of my pregnant best friend getting caught in the crossfire, so I begged off every invitation under the guise of fatigue. Which honestly, wasn't that far off. I was run down. Fucking exhausted.

Which was why Tate and I were curled up together on the sofa, watching a scary movie. It was the fifth or maybe even the nineteenth, in the franchise, but it was surprisingly good. And gory. Still, just hanging out with a guy and watching a movie was mundane, but completely unfamiliar territory to me. I didn't hang out with the men I slept with, hadn't since I realized everything they said was a lie to get more pussy. But with Tate, things were different. Maybe it was because he was easy to talk to or maybe it was just because he had no interest in impressing me, he was just Tate.

Or it could be that he fucked me so good I didn't give a damn about anything else. Including my appearance, as evidenced by the fact I was lounging around in nothing but a pair of cotton booty shorts and a thin tank without a bra. It was the definition of comfort, something I didn't often feel around men. Any men.

But Tate was all man and so far, I couldn't get enough of him. Which was a bit troublesome since we weren't dating. He was helping protect me and we were sleeping together. That was the sum total of our relationship and I was okay with that, even though things were starting to get...*confusing*.

I kept my gaze focused on the big ass TV where a man was begging for his life to no one in particular, but when another person appeared, I nearly jumped out of my skin. "Ass," I told Tate when he laughed at me.

"Sorry, but it's cute that you're scared of a made up thing on the screen when, you know, real life."

He was right, I was being a fool. But I enjoyed this kind of frivolous fear that went nowhere. "Have you ever had your face split into eight pieces by lasers? Because that looks like some very scary shit to me."

"Good point," he growled, one hand wrapped around my shoulders, his body crowding mine. His other hand, slid up and up my thigh so excruciatingly slow, my breath caught. "Don't worry, Cover Girl, I'll protect you."

I rolled my eyes at his words and tried for a snort that came out more like a breathless moan as his fingertips brushed my pussy through my shorts. Then he slid a finger past my wet panties through my swollen pussy lips. His thumb moved back and forth over my clit and one long finger rubbed all around my opening, teasing me mercilessly. "Protect me?" I panted.

"I'm distracting you from your fear, don't you know?" He chuckled lightly and finally, sweet Lord above, he stopped teasing me and slid a long finger deep, twisting and pumping until the only sounds in the room were my grunts and the sound of his finger plunging into my slickness.

"You're so fucking wet. Your pussy is always so wet for me."

My hips rolled against his hand and he added another finger, causing my hips to buck even harder. "Ooh, she knows what she likes, and you're it Golden Boy."

His deep chuckle vibrated through my body and I pulled him close, smashing our mouths together in a hot frenzied kiss that pushed me closer and closer to the edge.

"Good. I like her too," he purred against my lips and kissed me again. It was a hard kiss, rough and raw, like he would die if he didn't keep kissing me. Which was good, because if he stopped now I knew I would die from being too turned on.

His fingers sank deep and curved up as his mouth skidded down my neck and landed on a stiff, aching nipple. "Tate," I moaned as he sucked harder, his fingers moving faster and faster as I barreled toward orgasm. My hand reached out to his wrist, holding it still while I moved my hips fast and hard, fucking his hand as eagerly as he fucked me with his fingers. His gaze was dark with arousal, staring at me intently, watching for signs of pleasure.

A knock sounded at the door.

"Don't. Even. Think," I told him and my hips moved faster and faster as the knocking grew more insistent. "Oh fuck," I panted out when he added more pressure to my clit as the knocking grew louder. His teeth sank down into the soft, sensitive flesh of my nipple and that was enough to send me flying apart, clenching and pulsing around his fingers. "Damn, Tate. You do a body good."

He laughed and kissed me hard as the knocking was now an annoying fucking pest. "Glad to be of service."

I sighed with relief. "And I can't wait to service you," I told him. "As soon as we get rid of the uninvited guest." Fixing my shorts and shirt, I gave my hair a quick finger comb as I made my way to the door and yanked it open. As soon as I saw the dark uniforms, I froze. "What is it? Did you find them?"

"No, ma'am. We're not here about your case."

I frowned. "Then why are you here, at ten o'clock at night?"

The older uniformed officer stepped forward. "We have a complaint of an assault against Tate Ellison."

Arms crossed, I let out a bitter laugh. "Oh yeah, by who? And when exactly did this assault take place because I can guarantee you, he didn't do it." I felt Tate's heat when he came up behind me.

"It's fine, Teddy. I'll go clear this up."

"No! The last time you did the right thing, they put you in the slammer." His lips twitched and I smacked his chest. "This isn't fucking funny!"

"I know, but this is the easiest way to clear it up."

"How? With you already where they want you? No!" I turned to the cops. "He has a right to know who accused him and when, or else you might end up falsifying evidence. Again."

I waited for them to speak. Tate might want to do things their way, but I knew the power of a semi-hysterical woman on men, particularly men who pretended to be good men.

Finally, the older one with the paunch sighed. "Two nights ago, ma'am, but we can't release the name of the accuser."

"Whatever." I turned to Tate. "Tell me what you need."

"Call Bobby, she'll know what to do."

I nodded and squashed the jealousy that rose up in me. I'd seen the pretty attorney who looked like she baked cookies for fun and she'd been the perfect advocate for Tate.

"I'll take care of it," I whispered in his ear, taking a long lick of his sweaty, musky skin. "Keep your mouth shut," I warned.

"Got it," he assured me and stepped forward between the two cops.

The younger one turned with a sheepish smile and I shut the door in his useless fucking face. I took five seconds to freak the fuck out, letting my body work itself into a full-blown panic before I talked myself down from the ledge. Then I moved into action. Fresh from an incredible orgasm, my mind was clear and energized.

"Bobby," I said aloud and went to the little notebook that Tate kept beside the phone. I dialed the first one and got no answer, so I dialed the second one. "Bobby, this is a friend of Tate Ellison. He's been –"

"Miss, this isn't Bobby." A deep cultured voice spoke with a suggestion of an accent.

"Oh sorry, this is the number for Bobby Richardson, isn't it?"

"It is, but Bobby is indisposed at the moment," he said with a hint of a laugh that made it all clear.

"Well you can pass the message along." I took a deep breath and told him everything, including where Tate had been a couple nights ago and where he was now. "He needs someone with him now. I don't know how much you know but –"

He cut my words off. "I know everything, Miss."

"Teddy," I added. "Call me, Teddy."

"I'll let Bobby know."

"And she'll show up, right? Because I need her or you, someone to get their asses down to the station now!"

"Yes, Teddy, someone will be there."

"Great, thank you, whoever you are!" I disconnected the call, quickly dressed and scanned the area outside the house before I darted to the car, my heart racing so loud I couldn't hear the phone ringing on my next call.

"Hello?" Max's voice was groggy and thick with sleep.

"Max, wake up! The police just picked up Tate, something about an assault case. I've called his lawyer and I'm on my way to the precinct but I thought you'd want to know."

"What?"

"You heard me. See you." I ended the call, stepped on the gas and went as quickly as the laws of physics and the state of Nevada would allow. Tate was doing me a huge favor, taking my personal safety as his responsibility. It was something no one had ever done for me, not until I met Jana. That kind of unwavering loyalty and friendship deserved at least that much in return.

This fighting for him, I could do easily.

And I would.

Chapter 15

Tate

I should have fucking known this shit would happen, but I'd let myself get distracted. Get caught up in the day-to-day tasks of running a business, dealing with club business and Teddy. All of those distractions had made me forget who I was. Not just a man who'd spent six years in prison for a murder he didn't commit, but a man who, in the eyes of the two officers glaring at me, had won against the state. These assholes looked at me like I was already guilty, the same way they had right before they put handcuffs on me and pushed me through the system.

I was nothing more than a goddamn statistic to them. Well fuck them and fuck their statistics. I was the other number, the small number of men who'd been freed and deemed innocent. To these guys, that made me an enemy. A target. "Since your minds are already made up, I think I'll wait for my attorney to show up."

"That's fine." The young detective I'd come across once before, at the scene of Teddy's burned house, set out nearly a dozen photographs of a woman with a nasty black eye. Fucking Sheena. Troublemaking bitch. "We have the victim's statement and these fine images so I'll imagine you'll end up where you belong soon enough."

The other detective, the older one, Haynes, sighed heavily. "Look Mr. Ellison, this would all go a lot easier if you would just talk to us."

I nodded because he was right, it would. Too bad the hardest fucking lesson I'd ever learned didn't come at the hands of Uncle Sam, but the Las Vegas Police Department. "Still, I'll wait for my attorney."

Dodds, the young prick, laughed again. "The longer you take, the worse it'll be for you. Just tell us what happened. You get a little too rough for her? Or maybe she likes it rough and is now crying foul?"

I opened my mouth to say something, the rookie's eyes glued to my face, hopeful and arrogant. "Maybe you didn't hear me. I said, I am invoking my right to counsel."

He glared. "Just because you got out on a fucking technicality doesn't make you a good guy."

I sneered at him. "And just because the only way you can get your dick hard is to railroad innocent people, doesn't make you competent. Or good. *Officer*." These motherfuckers wanted me in a cage and they wouldn't rest until that happened. That was too bad because I would die before I let that happen. I would beat one of them to a pulp to ensure it, but I would never spend another night in a cage again.

"Innocent," he scoffed.

"Yeah, asshole, it's called DNA. Maybe you need to go back to the academy and figure out how this business of solving crimes works. You know, sometimes people lie."

He was pissed off now. "Yeah, they do."

Dark eyes narrowed to slits like that shit was supposed to intimidate me. It didn't. Yet I did bite down on my cheek to keep from cracking his fucking skull, but oh how I wanted to.

"I guess we'll see when my lawyer shows up." I sat quietly while Dodds was clunky in his attempt to get me to say something to incriminate myself. Dumb shit.

"Look Ellison, if it wasn't you, then we need find out who it was." Haynes was the good cop here and he tried hard to combat the damage his partner was doing. But I knew how to play the game.

"I'm aware of that, detective. But the last time I was honest and tried to help, you locked me up for it. My lawyer should be here soon." At least I hoped. This wasn't exactly Bobby's wheelhouse, but she'd gotten me out, so I hoped she could do something because I did not fucking relish the thought of sitting in a cell tonight.

"It'll be better for you," Dodds began but the door opened and a well-dressed man walked in like he owned the place.

"My client has said, at least a half dozen times, that he wished to remain silent until his lawyer arrived." He looked right at the rookie detective. "I'd hate to file more charges on civil rights violations. But I will."

Haynes stood, adjusting his oversized pants over his oversized belly. "We're just trying to clear a few things up, Mr. …"

"Mr. Gladstone. My client has an alibi for the evening in question, video surveillance starting at seven pm until after midnight, plus a sworn affidavit of his whereabouts thereafter. You have thirty minutes to verify it before I decide to make an example out of this department." The man took a seat beside me, calm as you please, and smiled. "We're waiting, gentlemen."

Chairs scraped against the linoleum as the cops stood and practically ran from the room. When we were alone, I turned to look him over. "Do I know you?"

"Gavin Gladstone. I work with Bobby and this is more my thing than hers, so I came. She's out there with your lady friend."

I blinked. "Teddy is here?"

He nodded. "She's a spitfire. Told me to 'get my ass down here and make those fuckers pay.'" I had to laugh at his cultured voice saying her words. "She gave me all the information I needed to get you out of here tonight. Don't worry."

I nodded at his words. "I wondered how you got everything so quickly. I figured the sun would be up before you got here."

"Divide and conquer. I was with Bobby when Teddy called. Bobby went to the casino and cashed in a favor to get the parking lot surveillance while my assistant and I came here to take Ms. Quinton's statement. And here we are."

"You really think I'm getting out tonight?"

"I'm certain of it. If not, you will add more money from the state of Nevada to your bank account. I would rather get you home, though."

"Damn straight," I added because there was nothing else to add. This man was one of those sharks you wanted when you got into trouble. He was the kind of lawyer cops feared, especially crooked ones. "Hey, you need more billable hours?"

"Always."

"Good, because I think we could use a guy like you." His only response was to slip me his card.

Thirty minutes later, Haynes opened the door with a sheepish grin. "You're free to go, Mr. Ellison."

I stood and shook his hand. "Thank you, detective." At Gladstone's surprised look, I shrugged. "He's been decent to me, which is more than I can say for any other pig in this fucking place."

"There are always a couple," he muttered and guided me out of the interrogation room and into the spacious pit where Teddy waited with Jana, Max and Bobby.

Teddy marched right up to me with a glare. "Well?"

I grinned and wrapped an arm around her shoulders, ignoring the confused looks of my brother and soon to be sister, as I told her about the assault. "It was Sheena. I don't know who, but someone fucked her up. Bad."

"That skank from your club?"

I nodded and she stepped away from my touch.

"You're free to go, though?" She looked to Gavin who nodded before she turned on her heels and marched to the parking lot.

Shit, she was pissed and I didn't want to deal with an emotional woman over some shit I didn't do. "Teddy, wait."

Max's hand landed on my shoulder and I stopped, but my gaze never left Teddy as she slid into her car and started the engine. I smiled when she waited instead of peeling out of the parking lot as pissed off women have been known to do.

"You good?" Max asked.

"I am now. I wished she hadn't worried you with this."

Max's look turned dark. "I'm glad she did. What's going on with you two?"

"Hell if I know," I told him and ran a hand through my hair, still mussed from Teddy's hands.

"Why don't you come to our place tonight?"

"Thanks, man but I just want to crash now. This shit has my head all fucked up and all I need is to be alone."

My gaze found Teddy's, even in the dark of night and through the dark windshield.

"That's not alone," Jana added, a smile in her voice.

No, it wasn't. Not at all, but funny enough, all I wanted was to be alone, with Teddy. "It's as alone as I want to be right now." With no more words for my family, I closed the gap between me and the pissed off, fuming woman in the car, slid into the passenger seat and waited for her to shift into drive.

When we got home she was still pissed, but after a long hot shower where she washed me gently, she climbed into bed beside me, naked, and I wrapped my arms around her.

It was the best fucking sleep I'd had in more than six years.

***

As soon as I opened my eyes, the previous fucking night came back to me in sickening clarity. How I went from having Teddy coming all over my hand to sitting inside a fucking interrogation room was still a haze but it didn't do anything to quell my shitty mood.

Even now, with Teddy's soft body and silky skin pressed against mine, I couldn't shake it off. So I did the only thing that could make me feel better. I lost myself in her body. Her back was pressed so tight against me, one tit resting in my hand, the tip hardening as my thumb brushed back and forth over it. The way she pressed back into me and moaned, even in her sleep, had my dick hard and ready. Angry and turned on wasn't exactly the mood I was going for, but when Teddy's back arched, bringing her wet cunt sliding across my stiff cock, I couldn't hold back.

I slid deep in one, slow thrust, groaning loud enough to finally rouse her from sleep. "Yes," she moaned in a throaty voice, one hand gripping mine right over her tits, a perfect handful. She was so tight from this angle, slick with arousal and so hot I couldn't control myself, pounding harder and faster in search of release. "Tate, baby," she moaned again, pumping her hips as one hand slid between her legs and fixed on her clit.

I could tell the second she started to play with her clit because her pussy pulsed around me, quivering as her breaths came in faster, shallower. "Let go," I grunted in her ear and she did, screaming as she fell apart, the orgasm hard and brutal, squeezing my cock so hard I had no choice but to ride the orgasm out. "Ah, fuck, Teddy!" My cock shot off like a rocket, pulsing and shooting deep into her wonderfully wet pussy.

"Not that I'm complaining," she panted, smiling at me over her shoulder, "but what was that all about?"

I didn't have an answer so I just shrugged. "You looked too fucking good to resist." It was partially true anyway, but I could tell by her expression she didn't believe me. Still, I slid from bed and walked to the bathroom where I lost myself in a long, hot shower. As the hot soapy water slid over my body, I ached to bury myself inside Teddy again, but I'd locked the door, ensuring that didn't happen. I needed some space today. The peace I'd found last night had evaporated. My mind was in a fucked up place and being around people would only end up making me angry. Well, *angrier*.

I stepped out of the bathroom and found the bed empty, but the sound of the shower in the other bathroom told me Teddy was up. I was just glad she hadn't decided to ambush me about locking her out of the bathroom. There was no need, because Teddy didn't cling.

Even still, I couldn't think about looking at her right now. She'd been a fierce advocate for me last night, making sure the system didn't fuck me over twice. And I was grateful as hell, but last night had brought home just how fucked up I still was over my time in prison. With the kind of anger pumping through me today, I knew I needed to get away, so I dressed quickly, grabbed my keys and helmet and jumped on my bike.

I rode and rode, trying to clear my mind of every goddamn thing haunting me. I pushed out the fucking cops determined to put me back in a cell. My brother's upcoming nuptials reminding me of the normal life not meant for me. Teddy and her fiery personality, sexy body and simple understanding and acceptance. I rode until my back ached and my hands cramped, my bike eating up the miles and miles of desert landscape. When I finally stopped for gas, water and some fresh air, I realized I was just a few miles from Reno.

Pulling out my phone on the side of the road as the sun began to set, I called the shop. "Hey Lasso man,

I need you to close the shop up tonight and open tomorrow. I'll catch up with you then."

"Sure thing, Golden Boy. Everything all right?"

I nodded even as my shoulders were rigid with tension. "Everything will be," I told him and ended the call, taking in several deep breaths of the cooler, crisper air.

Hopefully the distraction of a new place would clear my head.

Chapter 16

Teddy

I was a lot of things, but a woman who couldn't take a hint wasn't one of them. I knew the way he woke me up, with a deliciously hard fuck, that something was wrong. But when he locked the door as he showered, I knew it was more than that, and when I stepped back into the bedroom we'd been sharing and saw that his boots were gone, I didn't panic or freak out. Instead, I slowly got dressed, making sure I moisturized properly and looked out the window for what I knew I'd find.

Tate's bike was gone.

I took my time and shook off the disappointment of being fucked and discarded so easily. I should be used to it, but after so many years of taking control of my life, my destiny, it stung. Made me feel like the abandoned little girl in foster care all over again, and I just could not abide that feeling. Not fucking ever again. I packed my bags and loaded up my car and went back home.

To a construction zone. Not that I expected the contractors to perform feats of magic, but I really didn't want to think of so many people being inside my home. "I know I said I'd stay away but circumstances have changed."

Jase, the head contractor gave a sympathetic grin. "It's your house Ms. Quinton, but it would be safer if you used one of the other entrances. This flooring isn't quite ready for any weight yet." He sighed and met me in the back. "We should be no more than three more days."

"That's fine, Jase. I appreciate you guys fitting me in so quickly." I expected I might have to wait at least a month just to get them out, so I was happy they were almost done. "I'll be in my room."

My emotions were all over the place and my room was the best place for me, anyway. Body still humming from that good hard fuck from Tate, mind still reeling from how he could just walk away from me and I didn't even mean the sex stuff. It pissed me off that I'd let myself rely on someone else for my safety. I hadn't done that since I was ten and a half years old and realized I only had myself to rely on, and I hated myself for caring that he'd left.

But I did care, dammit. And that pissed me off more. But that was over; he'd made it more than clear that he was done with the burden of my personal security. One call to a local security company and someone had come out to do a consultation within the hour. I went with the Cadillac package, video surveillance, motion lights and a loud alarm system. If that didn't save me, nothing and no one would.

I spent the rest of the day getting my life back in order. Everything was all set for the engagement party, and after one final call to Mandy to check out the dessert spread, I felt pretty good about the party. I'd never thrown an engagement party at a biker gang hangout, but maybe it would expand my clientele. There was just this one thing to do and since I had no idea where Tate was, or if he was ever coming back, I called someone else.

"Hey Jag, sorry to bother you but I need you to send the invite for the party to Max and Jana."

He took a long pause before he responded. "Isn't Tate doing that?"

"He's gone and I need to make sure this gets done. Can I rely on you to do this?"

"Yeah, sure," he sighed. "I'll make sure they get it and that *both* of them show up."

"Thank you, Jag. You're the best."

"Yeah, yeah. Tell all of your friends. Please."

I laughed but before I could say anything else he'd ended the call. As I made my way down the never ending to-do list, I became aware of the house falling quiet as the contractors and then the security consultant knocked off for the day. The quiet grew louder, highlighting just how alone I was again and the creep factor set my stomach on edge.

Too wound up to eat, I decided to try and get some sleep, figuring unconsciousness would make the sounds less terrifying, or at least quieter. It didn't. Mostly because I couldn't get to sleep. I got up and went to the living room where I worked in front of the TV until I just couldn't keep my eyes open any longer. Two hours later and my fitful sleep was over.

Frustrated, tired and frightened, and thoroughly pissed off about it, I figured a shower and then a pot of coffee would help my body pick a side. Standing under the hot shower spray did help me wake up, but that only made my mind race with thoughts of the stalker's identity and what the hell had crawled up Tate's ass. But I reminded myself that he didn't owe me a damn thing. Basic human kindness would have been nice, but it wasn't the first time reality and my expectations had crashed violently. And I doubted it would be the last.

The sound of glass shattering sounded over the shower spray. What the fuck? Every nerve ending buzzed like I'd stuck my finger into a light socket. Then another shattering sound. And another. Was someone bombing my house?

The unmistakable smashing of glass was followed by the thuds of bricks or stones or other heavy objects. My heart jumped into my throat and I swore it stopped beating. I wasn't sure it was going to start up again. But then, my pulse began pounding like a madman. I was sure whoever was out there could hear it.

I knew I couldn't spend the rest of the night under in the shower, so I slipped out but left the water running to hide my movements and tiptoed across the bathroom floor. I pressed my ear against the door with my eyes squeezed shut. I hadn't heard anything after the last very heavy object hit the floor somewhere near the living room. No footsteps. No soft voices.

I held my breath and waited, listening for a few more seconds before I made my decision. I had to take action and decided to take a chance that I was alone. That the crazy fucker was outside and not in the hallway waiting for me to show my face. It was either that or spend the rest of my life in the shower.

SINFULLY SCARRED

I took the deepest breath ever, opened the door and vaulted over to the bedroom and grabbed the clothes I'd laid out off the bed and my phone off the dresser, then made a crazy-assed dash back to the bathroom. I locked myself in, images of some motherfucker letting loose an AR 15 through the bathroom door while I was making my hysterical call to the police. I dialed 911 and swore at my phone until the dispatcher answered.

"Someone is throwing things through my windows and I can't tell if they got inside the house or not."

I trembled against the wall, making sure I would be out of the line of fire from the window and the door while the 911 dispatcher assured me help was on the way.

I didn't believe her soft, soothing words but just the sound of them prevented me from freaking the fuck out any more than I already was as I pulled on my clothes. Her voice lulled me into a sense of false security that was quickly shattered when a loud pounding sounded that made me jump out of my skin.

"Ma'am it's the police, open up!"

The dispatcher heard them and gave me instructions. "It's okay Teddy. Ask for their names before you open the door."

I did and the dispatchers said, "It's all good. Those are the officers responding to this call. Open the door, sweetheart. You're all right."

I stood on shaky legs, my hands fumbling as I turned the little lock and twisted the doorknob. I pulled it open barely an inch and saw two tall men in uniforms. Police uniforms. They helped me to the sofa in the living room and ten minutes later my house was full again, this time with all manner of law enforcement.

They dusted for fingerprints. Picked up glass and bagged it. Asked me a thousand questions, took my statement and ninety minutes later they were gone.

And then, I was alone.

Again.

But this time, the two huge plate glass windows in the front of my house were broken along with all windows visible from the street. A cool breeze darting through the house was making me shiver. Tears welled up in my eyes as fear tried to overtake me again, the terror that had paralyzed me in the bathroom. But now I wouldn't let it. I refused to let those tears fall, because that wasn't me. I wasn't weak, but being around Tate too much had made me forget how strong I was on my own. I wouldn't cry. Not now, and maybe not ever. When this was over and the asshole stalker was caught, I'd worry about tears then. If I remembered.

For now, I had shit to do. Like call the contractor and ask him to price a shitload of windows when he arrived in a few hours. I wanted to call the security company and insist they install my shit right now, but that would probably only succeed in them taking their sweet ass time, so I scanned the empty house and went to my bedroom.

To unpack and then re-pack my bags. There were a few dozen hotels within spitting distance of my house and so many of them were luxurious and incredible so I decided that for the next week—at least—I would exile myself in luxury.

***

"I've been calling you for twelve fucking hours!"

I stared at the phone for a minute and then grinned. "Jana, it's nice to hear from you too."

"No! Dammit, Teddy, no! I went by your house yesterday and do you know what I found? Do you?"

"Uhm, my windows all busted out?"

"Your windows totally busted out," she replied as though I hadn't said a word.

"It's fine," I sighed. "The police are handling it, that's all they can do. In a few days I'll have a security system installed," I told her after glossing over the details of how my house came to be without windows. "No big deal."

"No big deal? Teddy, you need to tell me about this stuff. I'm your friend, hell you're like a sister to me and I need you to tell me when you're in danger like this. Please. I'm pregnant, not disabled."

I sighed and nodded even though she couldn't see me. "I got it, Jana. But you can't make me believe that keeping you and that little nugget of yours safe isn't the most important thing." She was finally getting the life she'd always wanted, the life she deserved, and I wouldn't let my drama interfere with that.

"And who else but you, Teddy, is going to think about my kid like that? We need you around, so stop keeping shit from me!"

I tried not to laugh because she was so clearly distraught, but there was something funny about it and we shared a good laugh. "Where are you staying?"

"A hotel with a good security team." The guys wore suits but you could tell them from other casino employees because they were all the size of gladiators. They all looked like former military bad asses and I felt safe. Safe enough, anyway.

"I don't like it. They care about you as long as you're inside the hotel, but what about work? What about walking you to your car? I'll call Tate."

"No, you won't." I didn't mean to use that harsh tone on her, but he was the last thing I needed.

"Where is he, anyway?"

I knew she would find out sooner or later. "I don't know. He left a few days ago. I guess I overstayed my welcome. I don't know Jana, but I don't want or need you to call him. I can take care of myself." If I'd remembered that sooner, I might have already had a security system installed at home.

Jana huffed her disagreement, damn near growling in her restraint. "I'll call him."

"I just said I can take care of my damn self!" Jana was talking but I couldn't listen any longer and disconnected the call, feeling guilty and pissed off. I wouldn't trust my safety to anyone else, not again. But none of that was Jana's fault so I called her back. "I'm sorry I yelled at you. But I meant what I said. I'll keep you informed if you trust my safety to me."

"I don't like it, but of course. Whatever you need to do. Did I mention that I don't like it?"

I laughed. "I know you don't, but I've been taking care of myself for a long time, girl. Thanks for worrying, Jana."

"Always."

"Good, now go get some rest. Love you."

"Love you too," she responded sadly, but I hung up before she could sate her curiosity with more questions about Tate. Questions I had no answers for and didn't really want to think about at the moment.

I had a quickie wedding tomorrow and Jana and Max's engagement party a couple days later. That and my personal security were the only things on my mind.

Certainly not some golden-haired biker who didn't know how to be a friend.

Chapter 17

Tate

Nothing made a man feel like more of a loser than knocking on a woman's door in the middle of the day and having her ignore you. Teddy's car wasn't in the driveway and her garage was empty, but there were workers in the house, which meant she had to come home regularly. Didn't she?

I'd been back from Reno for a few days and she hadn't answered any of my calls, not that I blamed her. I was an ass to her for no reason, and worse, I'd abandoned her when she needed my protection. Now she was determined to do without it, even if it compromised her safety. Stubborn damn woman.

As soon as Max called me in Reno, I hopped on my bike and returned to Mayhem as quickly as I could and found her things gone from my place, and her house vandalized. Again. And Teddy was nowhere to be found.

Not at her office, where a pretty young thing in a tight sweater had greeted me and told me she was in a consultation. An hour later another pretty young thing, this one in a short skirt said she was meeting with a vendor. Finally, a scrawny dude in hipster glasses said she was out to lunch. Yeah, I got the message loud and fucking clear, but that didn't mean I was giving up.

I sat outside in my car, watching as the three youngsters filed out of the office and locked up at the end of the day. Teddy still hadn't materialized but I didn't think she stayed away. There must be another entrance that she used. I could have laughed at the irony of her now using evasive techniques when I needed to find her. I called her again, hoping she would at least pick up and tell me to fuck off.

But she wouldn't. I knew she wouldn't, because of how I'd left. She was used to people not wanting her, particularly after her usefulness to them had run out, and I'd shown her that I was no different than countless foster families, social workers, agents, photographers — and men.

The phone rang in my hand and I grinned, thinking it was Teddy. "What's up?" I tried to sound casual, but the sound of my brother's voice pissed me off.

"Are you finally off your fucking period, man? Jana is stressing out so whatever the fuck you've done, fix it."

I laughed. "Based on these cramps, I think I might have another day or two of bleeding."

"Don't be a smartass, Tate. I'm serious."

Yeah I knew it. "I was an asshole. There's nothing to fix because she won't even answer my damn calls."

Max sighed but I could hear the frustration and stress he carried. "Mine either and now I know why. Jag sent us this invitation. You know anything about it?"

Jag? I should have known Teddy would let nothing or no one slow her down. I felt a small pang of ego at being replaced so quickly, but I knew it was unjustified. "I do. I know that you both need to be there, which is why I'll pick you guys up."

"That sounds good. What about Teddy, will she be there?"

There was no way she would miss this party, not when Jana was the only person she let get close to her. "I assume she will be, since she put it together." I let that piece of information hang in the air between us, hoping it would give him enough of a clue to understand why they both had to show up. It didn't matter though. I'd drag them to the clubhouse if I had to.

"Fine. Fix this shit with Teddy. Please."

Yeah, if only it was that fucking easy.

***

"You're really not going to tell us what this party is all about?" Jana was practically giddy in the passenger seat as we pulled into the parking lot at the clubhouse. The Reckless Bastards partied so much we rarely went all out except for weddings, funerals and the welcoming of new brothers. Tonight though, was special. While I'd been locked up, they'd worked hard to keep Max on this planet, so for him to find this happiness was reason enough to fucking celebrate.

"I'm really not. We're here, anyway. Show a little patience, Jana." I rolled my eyes, laughing when she smacked me in the chest. "Don't want to knock that baby loose."

She gasped in outrage, green eyes lit with amusement she tried to hide. "I can't believe you just said that about your niece or nephew."

"Yeah, yeah. Come on, Mom."

She stopped and looked up at me. "It's kind of creepy to hear you say that. Why do guys like being called 'daddy?'"

I blinked and then looked over at Max, who only shrugged. "Where does she get this shit?"

"Don't ask, brother. Just smile and nod."

I did as my older brother said, holding the door open so they could both enter before me.

"Oh my God! This is …" she looked back at me with a big smile and watery eyes. "Oh, Tate! This is incredible." She looked around, awe-filled green eyes taking in the decorations that I had to admit, looked spectacular. Everything looked like what could only be called biker princess heaven. Onyx chandeliers hung from above, chrome and black tables and chairs dotted the room and in the front were two bad ass biker thrones, complete with his and hers chalices. "You did this for us?"

I shrugged, uncomfortable with her bubbling emotions. "My idea but Teddy executed it all." And she'd done a damn good job. Better than I imagined in all the times we'd gone over the details. "She did a good job."

"A damn good one. Thank you," Jana wept and wrapped her little arms around me, squeezing tight. "Thank you, Tate."

"No problem." A quick look at Max told me he was just as grateful though not quite as gushy about it.

"Where is she?" Her blonde curls bounced around her shoulders as she scanned the room in search of her best friend, so excited she forgot to be self-conscious about the scar on her face.

Savior and Cross walked over to where we stood, smiling.

"Congratulations, you two." Cross hugged Jana and then Max. "Your friend is a bit of a whirlwind," he told Jana with an amused laugh.

Savior barked out a laugh. "That's an understatement. More like a drill sergeant! We could use her to train the prospects, though. She had them in top shape putting all this shit up." He shook his head and laughed. "Pissed off a few of the Bitches, too."

"That's my girl! So, where is she??" Jana was eager to thank her friend but I knew that some of her unease had to do with Teddy's recent troubles.

Cross shrugged and scratched his beard. "She left to go pick up the ice, even though I told her one of the prospects could do it. Now, drinks?"

Jana rubbed her belly and he snapped his fingers. "Teddy left some cider for you, plus I'm supposed to show you something if she's not here, and …" he looked around the room, seeing everything easily with the way he towered over everyone. "She's not, so follow me."

We all followed our club prez who ushered Jana to a big ass table filled with food. The centerpiece was a cake, four tiers with little sugary versions of Max and Jana. Her long blonde hair falling down the first two layers as Max tilted her over moments before their lips touched.

"Oh my God! This is so amazing! Babe, look at this, have I ever looked this hot?"

She was so excited she squealed, blowing out both of my eardrums.

"And look at your muscles, I don't know which of you is hotter."

She gave Max a heated look that left me a little uncomfortable to witness.

"I have to call her!" Jana walked away with her phone in her hand and a big smile on her face.

"You guys didn't have to do all this," Max said calmly as he stood beside me.

"I know, but I wanted to. Jana brought you back to life, gave you a reason to get right. I'll always love her for that. You deserve it, falling for a great woman doesn't happen every day."

He smiled, looking over at his bride to be with more love than I'd ever seen. "I've never met anyone like her. I just wish you could see that you deserve it too, no matter what stupid shit you're trying to convince yourself is true."

I shrugged, doing my best to look innocent as he slugged my arm. "I have exactly what I deserve." And I deserve exactly what I don't have too.

"Teddy, what's going on?" Jana's voice rose and the tension in her tone was palpable. "Just pump them.

Harder." She screamed as panic took over her voice. "Teddy, answer me! Teddy!" Jana turned to Max, sucking in shallow breaths as she began to hyperventilate.

"Look at me, Jana!" Hands on her shoulders, I stared into her eyes until she focused on mine. "Do what I do," I ordered and began breathing in and out slowly. She followed my instructions until she was calm, then I said, "Now tell us what happened."

"She was in the car and couldn't stop. It happened while we were talking. Something was wrong with her brakes. She hit them but the car didn't even slow down! I heard her crash. We have to find her!"

"Do you know where she is?" Max asked, worry and patience warring for priority on his face.

Jana shook her head. "No, she's hurt. We can't just leave her bleeding in a ditch somewhere! Come on, that fancy car has to have GPS!" She hung onto Max, her voice and eyes pleading with him to help her find her friend.

But she was right about one thing, we couldn't just leave Teddy to circumstance. "I'll go out and look for her along the routes to all the places that sell ice. You call 911, Jana and stay here with Max until we find her, okay? I'll check in with you guys."

She nodded absently, already dialing emergency services as tears streamed down her eyes. "Thank you, Tate. Find her, please."

"I will. I promise." I just hoped Teddy was in one piece when I found her. And I'd really like to know who in the fuck would have tampered with her brakes. I called Max as soon as I was on the move asking him about it.

"Cutting brakes isn't what you do to someone you want to be with, that's for someone you hate, right?"

Max grunted but I could hear the background sounds getting quieter as he moved away from the group. "Yeah. I thought for sure it was a former fan, but now I'm not sure."

"You think this is my fault? They wouldn't have been able to mess with her car if she'd been at the house with me." And that started my mind wandering to all kinds of places, like when had the brakes been fucked with and when?

"No, Tate. You were an asshole but this was going to happen at some point."

"Yeah, thanks," I told him and turned my focus to scanning both sides of the road, hoping like hell Teddy's car wouldn't be hidden in the dark shadows. I sent a prayer out into the world, pleading that if there was anyone listening, they would make damn sure Teddy was okay.

She had to be.

Chapter 18

Teddy

Before I even woke up, I knew something was wrong. The first thing I noticed was the bleachy, disinfectant scent that told me I was in some type of medical facility like a hospital or maybe an insane asylum. At this point I had no idea. Then I heard the *beeps*, the *whirs*, *hisses* and *clicks*, all telling me that the pain I felt meant something bad had happened. My eyes wouldn't open, like lead weights were keeping the lids closed no matter how hard I struggled.

Finally, I gave up and just listened to the sounds of all the machines monitoring everything from my heart rate to blood pressure and even the amount of oxygen in my blood. Between the pain darting all around my body and the number of different sounds all around me, I knew I was hurt. Bad. And as I tried to sit up, the shooting pain in my arm brought it all back to me.

Driving back to the Reckless Bastards hangar with a trunk full of ice, because ice was another thing Tate was supposed to do. Only he'd been off doing who and what the fuck was anybody's damn guess, and that was how I'd ended up on Interstate 15 at seventy-five miles an hour. The car started to vibrate and then made a kind of burp as I moved over for the next exit, but then Jana called, distracting me. Still, I listened to her excitedly ramble on about all the things she loved about the party, smiling at her over the top happiness.

The car wouldn't slow down as I turned onto the exit ramp. Pumping the brakes as hard as I could and realizing something was wrong. Telling Jana. Going too fast on the exit and then the asphalt turning to grass and mud. A sharp smack and everything went black.

So, I wasn't dead and this hospital room was my personal hell. I put all of my focus and concentration on opening my eyes. Fucking blinding white fluorescent lights made it hard, but I was determined to get answers and then get the fuck out of this place.

Finally, when my eyes opened, I scanned the room to confirm it was a hospital room and not a torture dungeon. But when I tried to sit up, fiery nails stabbed every inch of my skin.

"Oh fuck!" A string of colorful curses rang out in the empty room as I tried to reach for the call button. Some genius had put it on the same side as the arm snug in a fucking cast.

"Shit, shit, goddammit! Got you fucker." One finger landed on the call button for about four seconds because that's all I could handle before the pain intensified.

"Ms. Quinton, you're awake."

Thank you, Captain Obvious. "Yes, can someone tell me what happened?"

"You were in an automobile accident and the police are waiting to speak with you." The nurse hesitated and I glared, hoping she wasn't seriously going to put the needs of the police before my own medical needs. "Right. You sustained no significant injuries other than the broken arm and sprained wrist. There are some cuts and bruises and a possible concussion, but all things that will heal in no time. I'll let the doctor know you're awake."

I frowned at the nurse's retreating back, feeling uneasy and okay, maybe a little scared, too. What else did the doctor need to tell me if I was completely healthy but with a few minor injuries? I felt myself begin to freak out as I reached down to my leg with my good arm, not really relaxed even though I didn't feel any screws or other damage to my already impaired leg.

Thankfully, I didn't have to worry too long. A few minutes later the doctor, a petite woman with long black hair and blunt cut bangs, strolled in with a professional smile. "Hello, Ms. Quinton, I'm Dr. Evans. How are we feeling?"

I sighed, centering myself so I could deal with another medical professional. "I'd prefer it if you just tell me exactly what's wrong in the simplest way for me to understand. I don't need false hope and I don't need my feelings to be spared, Doc."

Something like pride flashed in her eyes and she nodded at me. "Okay then. Nurse Bellows gave you the highlights, but the most limiting thing will be your arm and maybe the sprained ankle. I'll give you some painkillers that won't have a negative impact on the baby, and we'll monitor you for another night until we're sure about that concussion." Dr. Evans' mouth was still moving but I couldn't hear her words anymore.

Baby? She said the painkillers wouldn't negatively affect the baby. A baby? "What baby?"

She frowned for a second, and then her face changed to a more understanding look. "You didn't know? Based on your hormone levels, you're about nine weeks along."

"Nine weeks? How did I not know?" My heart moved up to my throat and I took a deep breath to calm the dizziness in my head. Pregnant? How could I be? Tate? No way. We'd always used protection.

"Life," she said with a sympathetic smile and a shrug.

"Is the baby okay? Was it harmed in the accident? What do I need to do?" I was freaking out for sure, but this news combined with everything else, was about to push me over the edge. A girl could only take so much.

Dr. Evans smiled and laid a hand on my shoulder. "All you need to do is take your prenatal vitamins, rest and eat better than you've ever eaten in your life. Well balanced meals and exercise, once that ankle is healed."

"Thanks, Doc. I can handle that," I lied.

"Good. Are you up to speaking with the police, because they've been waiting to speak with you."

I nodded as my thoughts swirled. Single and pregnant, just like my own mother. But unlike dear old dead mom, I also had a stalker in the mix. Because you could take the girl out of the ghetto, but you couldn't take the ghetto out of the girl.

"Give me ten minutes and then send them in?"

"Okay, I'll let them know."

I let out a long sigh and thought about Jana and the party. It was time for me to do better.

Chapter 19

Tate

"Is she all right? What happened?" I was on my feet and moving across the dimly lit waiting room as soon as Jana stepped through the door.

"She's a little banged up, Tate, but she's fine. I didn't get to stay long because the cops are in with her. They're pretty sure her car was tampered with."

I couldn't swallow past the lump in my throat at hearing that someone had done this to her. "This is all my fucking fault." I put an arm around Jana and led her to the seat beside Max, who watched his woman with worry in his eyes.

Jana groaned and smacked my chest. "Yeah, Tate, this is all about you."

I grinned at her show of levity, appreciative. "Seriously, I was an ass. Got too much in my own damn head and just walked out while she was in the shower. She knew what the fuck I was doing, probably better than I did at the time, and so she went home. Giving whoever this asshole is, a perfect chance to target her." It pissed me off that I let those fucking cops get inside my head, because this was the end result.

Jana sighed and grabbed my hand. "Teddy is her own woman, Tate. We offered her a place to stay and she refused us too. This psycho is out to get her so what's important is that we find him! Or *them*." She shook her head as tears fell down her cheeks. Max wrapped his big arms around her and I stepped back, looking out the window as fat, round drops of rain fell to the ground.

All I could think about was it was a good thing the accident had happened before the rain came or else her injuries might have been worse. It wasn't much to be grateful for, but all of it seemed too perfect, or too perfectly timed.

"Shit, of course!"

Jana and Max's gaze both found mine and I chuckled, walking out of the waiting room in search of Teddy.

Teddy who was ignoring me and had no desire to see me.

Well she would now, because her safety depended on it. She was buried in pillows gazing through the half-closed blinds when I walked in, so lost in thought she didn't even hear me enter. "Teddy. I'm glad you're all right."

She tensed and slowly turned her head so I could see the anger and hurt, the disappointment in her big, blue eyes. "Tate. I'm fine." She pulled the covers up to her chin with her one good hand.

I grinned. "Sorry sweetheart, but not from where I'm standing."

"I'm also not your problem." She spit out. It really was too bad that she couldn't cross her arms because the defiant tilt of her chin was adorable. And sexy.

"I can understand why you think that, and you have every right to be pissed off and ignore me all you want. But later. Right now, I need to keep you safe."

She groaned.

"No, don't say anything. You're not a problem. Ever. So tell me Teddy, are you going to shut up so I can apologize or are you going to answer my questions?"

I could see the indecision in her eyes. She wanted me to apologize and to mean it, but she'd never do anything that might resemble asking for an apology.

"Ask your damn questions."

I grinned at her fiery temper. A redhead to her core. "Okay. I need you tell me everything that happened from the moment you left my house."

"After you disappeared, I packed my things and went home. The workers were still there and I got a few things done, including a security consult." She went on and on about the mundane tasks that filled her day and when she got to the breaking glass, something became clear.

Someone had waited until she was as vulnerable as possible to maximize her terror. "Have you noticed anyone following you, or seen the same car in different, random places?"

She shook her head, wincing and pinching her eyes closed at the pain. "No. And I have been looking, being cautious and even taking different routes."

I smiled because she was actually listening even though she'd pretended not to at the time. "When did you notice something was wrong with your car?"

"Not until maybe a minute or two before I realized something was wrong. The noise wasn't noticeable, not really, so I turned down the radio to listen. It vibrated a little more and then the brake pedal went down too easy but nothing happened." She was starting to get upset, remembering and I felt like an ass all over again. "I've been busy, Tate. Between the party, the work on my house and the psycho stalker, I've been a little preoccupied."

"No one is blaming you, Teddy. I'm sorry I left the way I did and I know you won't believe me, but it had nothing to do with you. Spending time in there with the cops did a number on my fucking head and I had to get away."

"Sure," she snorted, which told me clearly what she thought of my apology. Or my excuse, I wasn't really sure. "It doesn't matter, Tate. You don't owe me anything. Including an apology."

She wouldn't listen, not now. But that didn't mean I'd give up. If we were nothing else, Teddy and I had become friends and my behavior had betrayed that friendship. "Maybe I don't, but I want to be a better person than that for you. You deserve more."

She scoffed. "I have exactly what I deserve, Tate. Believe me."

I didn't believe it, but I knew arguing the point with her now would only make her angrier. "How long are they keeping you?"

"At least another night. I might have a concussion and since I have no one to watch me safely, they're keeping me." Her words weren't accidental, we both knew it, but I don't think she meant it to hurt. To Teddy, it was just a fact.

"And?"

She shrugged. "I have a sprained ankle and a broken arm, so I'll take the rest of today to figure something out. You should probably go check on Jana and Max."

"They weren't in a fucking car accident!"

"Don't yell at me, Tate! Who fucking asked you to come, anyway?"

There was the fiery beast I knew she hid within her. "Not you, because you would never admit such a weakness as needing someone, would you?"

"What would be the point of needing people when they just leave? I'll stick with myself since I know I won't let me down." She sucked in a deep breath, her pain written in every line drawn across her face. Watching her struggle to reach the call button tore me up and I went to her, placing it in her hand.

"Thanks," she growled at me, clearly not thankful.

"I won't let you down, Teddy. You might hate me forever, but I promise I won't ever let you down again."

She yawned. "Hating you wouldn't help anything. Don't worry about me, worry about yourself." I guessed me being here exhausted her because her voice got weak as she drifted off to sleep.

I stood to leave just as a nurse was about to enter with a tray full of nurse shit. I held the door for her and watched as she walked over to sleeping beauty. She must not have realized Teddy was in la la land because I heard her say, "Ms. Quinton, we have painkillers for you that won't harm the baby! And of course your prenatal vitamins." Her voice was chipper but her words sounded so foreign I figured I had to be experiencing a fatigue-induced hallucination.

Because if I wasn't, then that nurse just said Teddy was pregnant.

Only Teddy hadn't said a word to me about it.

Because the baby wasn't mine? Or, because I wasn't the kind of man she wanted to raise a child with?

Chapter 20

Teddy

"God it feels so good to be going home." At least it would be if they'd let me out of here.

I tried to explain to Jana that I couldn't wait to leave those blinding lights behind, the noise of the machines and the constant interruptions by nurses coming in to poke and prod me just when I'd finally get comfortable. But Jana wouldn't get off my case.

"Oh no, Theodora. Don't think you can just drop a bomb like, 'I'm pregnant' and change the subject." Arms crossed over her own growing belly bump, she sent me a narrow-eyed gaze that was supposed to intimidate me.

"You're actually *pregnant*?" she whispered. "Like a bun in the oven, fetus growing into a squiggling little baby in your belly, you're gonna be a mommy, pregnant?"

This girl was way too excited for the little bit of sleep I got last night. "Duh. Is there another type of pregnant I don't know about?"

She rolled her eyes, but my best friend could not contain her excitement. I'd bet a million dollars it had little to do with me and everything to do with the fact that she wouldn't have to do this alone. "Oh my God, this is the best news ever! We're pregnant! Together! Mostly at the same time. And by brothers!" Her squeal was so high pitched I had to plug my ears.

"Settle down before they start evacuating patients because of that tornado siren you call a voice." She wore a sheepish smile and then burst out laughing and pulled me in for a tight, loving hug.

"Okay, Hormones McCrazy," I told her as I extracted myself from her surprisingly strong grip. "Because you're not going to like the next part."

She froze, her green eyes going wide. "You're not keeping it?"

"Jana," I sighed.

"Foster care isn't ideal, but we came out all right. Didn't we?"

"Jana! I'm keeping my baby, but I'm swearing you to secrecy."

She was my best friend and I knew asking her not to tell Tate's brother and her future husband wasn't right, but this time, I felt okay about being selfish.

Jana sighed, completely deflated from her giddiness a few moments ago, and shook her head. "I love you, Teddy, but I'm not sure I can keep this from Max."

I glared at her, not surprised but disappointed anyway. "Then we have nothing else to talk about." The room had fallen silent, tension thickening the air as I busied myself packing up my few things.

"That's not fair, Teddy! You can't ask me not to say anything to him!"

"Say what to who?" Max asked, leaning against the doorway as cool as you please. I didn't think for one second that he hadn't heard the full conversation because he was as inscrutable as they came.

"Nothing to no one, because there's nothing to say. To anyone." I turned my back to them, wishing I'd just called a damn cab even though I couldn't count on a cabbie to help me move around with one good arm and one good leg.

"You both are shitty liars," Max said and even though my back was to him, I could hear the smile in his voice. "For the moment, I'm okay with that because I'm ready to get the fuck outta here."

Join the club. "I've been ready since they wheeled me in here, unconscious and broken, but it'll be a few more hours. You guys should probably go and I'll get myself home." As bitchy as it sounded, if I couldn't share my thoughts and secrets with my best friend, I didn't see any point in having them here.

"Cut the shit, Teddy." Max lowered his big body into one of the hard plastic chairs and pulled it so he was between me and the doorway. I wanted to think it was a protective move but the intensity of his gaze said it was more of a *keeping me here* move. "What's this big secret?" He smiled and I said nothing so he shrugged. "You know Jana's gonna tell me, don't you? She might just break from the silence, or I really hope she makes me coax it out of her." He smiled and looked over at Jana with love and heat in his eyes.

I held up a hand, fake gagging. "Oh please, spare me the damn details, Max." I knew I couldn't hide the pregnancy from Tate forever, but I needed to come to terms with it myself before he started trying to tell me what to do with my body and my life. I didn't need more opinions before I decided for myself, but I knew Max was right about one thing, Jana would break before the day was over. Time for a subject change. "Please tell me you guys got to eat some of the party food?" I'd spent so much time planning that party, I really hoped it wasn't for nothing.

That perked Jana right up, hopefully her impending betrayal all but forgotten as she gushed over the cake, the cupcake tower, the mac & cheese balls, the bread bowls filled with dips.

"It was so beautiful and so delicious! Some of the, uhm…club girls, brought some of it to the waiting room so plenty of people got to enjoy it, Teddy. I can't," she blinked and sniffed, trying to fan away the tears threatening to drop. "I can't thank you enough for the party. It was a shock, the best surprise really, and so great. Until you nearly died."

"I'm happy for you both, and it was my pleasure. But this was all Tate, I just put it together."

"You have to forgive him sometime, Teddy." That came from Max, a dark scowl on his face as he stood to make room for the doctor and nurse entering my room.

"There's nothing to forgive, Max. He was helping me and then he wasn't. No big deal. I'm a big girl and I have been taking care of myself for a really long fucking time." Even if I did let myself forget for a little while. Max and I were trapped in a staring contest until the nurse checked me out while the doctor gave me orders for wound care, painkillers and walking.

"It'll be difficult at first, but we have a wheelchair to help you get around. But only short trips, like the bathroom," the doctor emphasized. "And here are your prescriptions. Feel free to call if you have any questions." I smiled, grateful she hadn't accidentally spilled my secret.

Finally, I was free to go home. The drive was short and silent, but I didn't care. I just wanted to stumble to my sofa and get lost in a few days of Netflix bingeing.

"Fuck my life," I groaned as Max stopped in my driveway where Detectives Haynes and Dobbs waited. With Tate.

"You have to deal with them some time," Jana offered, most unhelpfully.

"Actually, I don't." It was a struggle, but I managed to get out of the car without any help. But Max wasn't moving all that quickly so I stood, wobbling on one leg and trying like hell not to fall. I watched Max yank the chair from the back of his truck and struggle to open it. "Bring it here."

He ignored me, still fumbling with it and letting out long strings of colorful curses. "Fuck this shit. Tate," he yelled and motioned to me.

"I don't need any help. I need the goddamn wheelchair," I yelled, holding a hand up to stop Tate's movement and nearly toppling over as I grew unsteady.

But what did it matter what I wanted with two overbearing men around? Tate scooped me off my feet and carried me up the steps, leaning down so I could unlock the door and disarm the new security system. Ignoring Tate and his big strong arms, I looked around my house and noticed there were no traces of any of the shit that had gone down here over the past few months. No paint cans, no soot, no broken glass.

No fucking gifts.

He set me on the sofa and I winced.

"Sorry."

I brushed off his apology. "It's fine. It hurts constantly anyway."

"I know and I'm damn sorry for it," he bit out, hurt and anger flashing on his handsome face. He looked and sounded sorry, but I was angry, in pain and really bitchy, so basically not in a very forgiving mood.

"Don't be."

He frowned. "How can I not? I promised to —"

I cut him off. "You don't owe me anything, Tate. I'm grateful for the help you gave me, but I'm not your responsibility so don't let this hang on your conscience."

With a frustrated grunt he dropped down beside me on the sofa. "I think I know who's been doing this."

I tensed but refused to overreact, so I took a few deep breaths and pushed out all the *what ifs* running through my mind. "Tell me."

"Her name is Sheena," he said, but I only shrugged because the name didn't ring a bell.

"She's a Reckless Bitch and she's made it clear since I got free that she wants me."

I scoffed. "I knew you fucked her, there was no reason to lie about it."

So typical. Men lied even when they were getting sex without strings, and that was why they couldn't be trusted.

"I never fucked her." He growled the words at me, his eyes fierce and begging me to believe him.

I didn't.

"She's ready to be somebody's old lady and she figured I was it. Then she found out about you."

"This started before we ever did anything."

He nodded, his face in a twisted plea. "But she doesn't know that. All she knows is that she's seen us out having dinner together. Planning the engagement party and self-defense."

I leaned back on the sofa, exhausted because it all made sense. Tate and I had been spending a lot of time together and to a crazed outsider it probably did look like we were a couple.

Before we could take it any further, the detectives entered with Jana and Max trailing behind them, sheepish looks on everyone's downturned faces. "Does this mean you got her?"

Detective Haynes stepped forward and raked a hand through his hair, the universal sign for bad news. "No. We haven't been able to locate the suspect. No one has seen her since the party." He blew out a frustrated breath and I could see that he really was one of the good cops. "We can send a car around hourly, but if there's an emergency …" he stopped, unwilling to finish the sentence.

"I'm on my own," I finished for him and he nodded. It wasn't his fault but that didn't change how I felt. "Then I hope the next time I see you, I'm still drawing breath since I'm in no position to protect myself. Have a good evening, detectives."

Haynes glanced around the room and I knew what was coming. "Can't you stay with someone?"

"Nope," I said immediately before Jana or Tate or Max could say a word. After a long stare-off, the detectives left.

"If someone can put the wheelchair next to the sofa and lock it, all I need is water and a few snacks." Because of my arm, crutches wouldn't work. And I was grateful the physical therapists in the hospital helped me practice getting in and out of the wheelchair one-armed by myself. The snacks turned out to be leftover engagement party food, which made me giddy. I was good to go. Or as good as I'd ever be. I mustered a smile. "Thanks, Jana."

She wrapped her arms around me and kissed my cheek. "I wish you would come stay with us." With a quick glance down at my belly she stepped back, her green eyes pleading with me.

"I'll be fine, girl. Get some rest." Surprisingly, Max bent over to hug me too. I thought he only tolerated me because of Jana, but maybe I was wrong. "Thank you for your help, both of you." I meant it but wanted them out of there because all of sudden I was tearing up. "GO!" I said with a harsh laugh, and they left.

And then there were two. Tate was itching to say something, had been for the past fifteen minutes so I sat there and fought down the emotion that Jana and Max had stirred up and just waited. And waited.

Then he put it all on me. "Ready to talk?"

After he was the one who'd walked out on me? I felt like a teenager throwing a hissy fit. I crossed my arms and pouted but didn't give a shit how dumb ass it looked. "No, but you have me at a disadvantage since I can't get up and walk away."

"Would you walk away right now if you could?"

"Damn right I would, Tate. I'm tired, I'm sore, all broken up and possibly in danger. I'd like a hot bath and to sleep in my own bed, thank you very much, but none of that is going to happen now, so just fucking talk if that's what you want. Or else leave."

My chest heaved, the pain shot up and down my body, not even the adrenaline of anger was enough to bury the pain. "Besides," I started, trying to sound much calmer, "what do we have to talk about?"

He leaned forward and settled his angry gray eyes on me. "How about the fact that you're pregnant with my baby?"

Yeah, there was that.

Chapter 21

Tate

I knew I'd shocked Teddy but she was a pro, her emotions carefully in check and her face gave nothing away. There was a lot of bat-shit crazy shooting through her head if she thought for one damn second I'd let her keep a child from me. "Now you have nothing to say?"

She blinked, her long eyelashes moved slow and deliberate. "What are you talking about?"

"Seriously, Teddy? That's how you want to do this? Fine, I heard the nurse tell you she brought your prenatal vitamins." That was three days ago and yet, she hadn't told me anything.

"You must have misheard," she offered simply. But she didn't say anything else, refusing to answer even basic questions about her pain levels as she reached over to the end table for a book and pretended to read a murder mystery. An hour later she'd given up the pretense and dragged her laptop off the coffee table, wincing in pain rather than ask me for her help, and checked her email. Then, she called her employees and let them know she was homebound for the foreseeable future and issued orders like a drill sergeant.

I sat right beside her the entire time, watching TV or playing games on my phone, waiting for her to relent. She never did. Not even when the pizza and wings I ordered arrived. She extended her good arm beyond the point of pain to reach for her food, rather than ask me.

"Damn stubborn woman," I growled, slamming two slices and a few wings onto her plate.

"Thanks," she murmured and inhaled the food. Teddy didn't say another word to me. After eating her fill, she took a pill and fell asleep nestled into the corner of the sofa. By the time she woke up, it was nearly dinnertime.

I held a glass of water out to her so she could take her pills. "How's your pain?"

She snorted. "I'll take the pills without the small talk, thanks."

"Dammit Teddy, you're having my baby. You might hate me, even though it kills me to think it, but we are having a kid together. This is just one more reason for us to be together."

She flashed an angry glare up at me. "There is no *us*, Tate. I made that mistake but only for a moment. Luckily for you, it's easy to fix."

"It's not a fucking mistake, Teddy."

She nodded, suddenly more confident and sure. "It was, Tate. You know it was, because you walked away first."

"I said I was sorry." I never expected Teddy to be the unforgiving type, she'd always seemed so laid back.

"But that's just it, I don't want your apology. You made me forget, at least temporarily, that I needed to rely on myself. It was a nice little vacation, but if I'd remembered it maybe I wouldn't be defenseless right now." She shook her head with a smile but there was no joy behind it. "I don't want or need your guilt. We had fun."

Just when I didn't think I could feel any worse, she said the one thing guaranteed to slice me open. Being with me had reminded her that she couldn't rely on other people. That meant she wasn't ready to hear everything else I had to say. Not yet, anyway. "We're not done talking about this," I warned her but she looked up at me, almost bored.

"Yes, we are. I'd like you to leave."

"Fuck that! I'm not leaving you alone. Hate me all you want, but I can't let anything happen to you, Teddy. I just fucking can't."

She didn't respond, just diverted her gaze back to the television, dismissing me. She didn't think she could rely on me and I couldn't blame her even though it pissed me off to no end.

I'd leave, but not without making sure she was taken care of. I dropped down and roughly kissed her cheek. "See you soon, Teddy."

She grunted and that only made me smile wider as I walked out to my truck and made a few calls. Teddy thought she could get rid of me easily but she was wrong.

So, so wrong.

Cross picked up my call on the fourth ring. "What's up, man?"

"Can we call a meeting? I have some shit we need to discuss. Important shit." I knew the Reckless Bastards were a brotherhood, though some people called us a gang, and that meant our first priority was to each other and our families. But Sheena was technically part of that family so I had to tread carefully.

"You on your way now?"

I started the engine and reversed out of Teddy's driveway. "Yep. See you in ten." It was time I remembered who the fuck I was, and what I was willing to do for those I cared about. And though she wasn't ready to hear it, I cared about Teddy.

I might even fucking love her.

Chapter 22

Teddy

"You don't have to stay here, Lasso. What the hell kind of name is that, anyway? And doesn't a man with a name and a face like yours have someplace else to be?"

Not that I didn't like his company, the man was funny and charming, and that Texas twang was inviting.

"There's always someplace else to be, Teddy. But when a brother is in need, we're all in need. Besides, this is probably the only date we'll ever have."

I couldn't help but laugh at his broad-shouldered confidence. "Is this a date?"

"You've got me. Food and a beautiful woman, what else do we need?"

"Murder," I said seriously, laughing when his hands went to his crotch. Then I pressed play and queued up a new murder documentary that had just been released. "Now the date is perfect."

He laughed but ten minutes in, Lasso was antsy and I paused the TV and looked at him. "What?"

"Are you okay?"

"Yeah, but this shit? It's creepy as fuck." He shook like a kid with the heebie jeebies, so I switched to a standup comedy special.

We laughed way too loud and too hard, but for seventy-five minutes I was able to forget the shit show that was my life. "You're not a bad date, Lasso."

He flashed that beautiful smile and batted his eyelashes. "Spread the word around, would ya, sweetheart?"

I couldn't help but laugh. "I'm sure you have no trouble getting dates."

"Not at all, but word of mouth is the best reference."

I laughed so hard I cried. "I cannot believe you just said that." I couldn't stop laughing because he was as outrageous as he was handsome and charming. "I really pity the women of Las Vegas."

"You should pity yourself, darlin'. You're the one who can't have any of this." He rolled his hips in what was supposed to be a sexy laugh and I shook my head.

"I think I'll survive, Lasso. Besides I can't remember the last time I had a big handsome friend. You'll be great to shop with. All the women will flock to you and I can pick up all the good shit on sale."

His deep laugh was so loud we barely heard the knock at the door. I froze. Immediately, my thoughts went to the woman who wanted me out of the picture. I laughed bitterly. If only she knew that he was no more mine than hers. "I'll get it," he said and stood to head for the door.

"Wait!" I reached for my tablet and pulled open the camera app, turning it to him. "It's Jag." The new security system was up and working just as it should. Of course my mind had already spun eight different scenarios that Sheena could use to bypass it. Hell, if the event planning thing didn't work out, I had a future as a security specialist.

"I'm here to relieve the beast," Jag said with a smile as he walked in, flashing a wink at me over Lasso's shoulder.

Lasso looked back at me with his most charming smile. "Look at Jag, here again for my sloppy seconds."

The handsome, dark-skinned man grinned. "You fuck everyone Lasso, every woman in Las Vegas is your sloppy seconds. No offense, Teddy."

"None taken, Jag. Come on in. We have some leftover Peking duck if you're hungry. Babysitters get fed in this house." That thought made my stomach hurt as it occurred to me that soon I would have to think about things like babysitters.

Maybe.

If I ever dated again.

"I didn't sign up for babysitting," Jag said. "I'm here because I heard a pretty girl needed some company."

"Geez, do they teach you all how to charm girls out of their panties during your biker gang orientation or something?"

Both men turned to me, an affronted look on their face. "Biker gang? Orientation?" Lasso's big meaty hands were on his hips as he attempted a glare.

"Or *something*, I said. Didn't you hear that part?"

Jag laughed, did some fancy goodbye handshake with Lasso and pushed him out the door. "How are you feeling, Teddy?"

I shrugged and leaned my head against the arm of the sofa, and when I woke up again the sun was shining and yet another biker was looking at me with concern in his eyes.

"Another one," I groaned. "Which one are you?" He looked familiar, mostly it was the beard, but the pain pills had me so groggy I couldn't remember.

"I'm the best one. They call me Savior."

"Right. Blue-eyed Jesus." He barked out a laugh and put an ice-cold bottle of water in my hands. "Thank you."

"No problem. Do you need to get up or anything? Hit the head, maybe?"

These guys, despite how tough and badass they all looked, they were all sweethearts. "I can manage it on my own, but thanks. You are strictly here to babysit me, I suppose." I didn't know why Tate, or maybe Jana had convinced Max to recruit his club members to watch out for me, but it was annoying.

And nice.

"Not babysit. A brother asked us to keep you and the baby safe so that's what we're doing."

"Big bad biker boys don't babysit?" I arched a brow at the stoic man and his lips quivered beneath his beard.

"Exactly."

Savior was a quiet guy so aside from some nervous hovering when I made a couple trips to the bathroom, we mostly sat in silence. He flipped between sports and news on the TV while I did as much work as I could on my laptop with just one hand. It was an exercise in frustration.

And that was pretty much how the rest of the week went. Various Reckless Bastards showing up on my doorstep, most of them bearing food and some bearing booze I couldn't drink because of the pills. Because of the baby. I tried to work but it never lasted for more than fifteen or twenty minutes. Having a sprained wrist and a broken arm didn't just hurt like a son of a bitch, it was damned inconvenient.

After the third day, I'd moved to my bedroom. To my fluffy, pillow-topped mattress and my blessed pillows, the feather ones and the memory foam. Soft, cool cotton sheets. Candles. It was my favorite room in the house and it was now my refuge. I stayed in bed all day and night, mostly listening to music because there was nothing else to do. I couldn't work or cook or clean, and I couldn't walk.

The phone rang nonstop and even though I had no desire to talk to anyone, I answered Jana once a day just to keep her from going crazy. The detectives never called so I assumed it meant that Sheena was still out there, waiting to make her next move. Tate didn't call and honestly, it sucked but it didn't bother me as much as it should have. Nothing bothered me, really. I ate because I knew the little guy or girl in my belly needed it, not because I was hungry.

And on the day of my doctor's appointment, morning sickness kicked in like a professional soccer player. I slowly got dressed, lying down and breathing deeply in between bouts of nausea until I could stand again. I slipped on my shoes, still breathing deep, as I made my way to the front of the house to wait for Jana.

Instead, I got Tate.

"Sorry to disappoint you, but Jana's morning sickness is out of control. She asked me to take you." I hated that he looked so pained by my mask of indifference, but I did not want to care about his pain.

"I'm not disappointed, just surprised that no one thought to call me about last minute changes. No big deal."

"That's what your mouth says, but your face says different."

"My face says that I've been puking my guts up all morning, Tate. Nothing more." And now that we were on our way to the one place there was guaranteed to be no food, I was hungry. This pregnancy was determined to kick my ass.

He turned to me at a red light, grey eyes all dark with worry. "Is everything all right? You'll talk to the doctor about it?"

I sighed. "It's morning sickness, Tate. Same as Jana. Allegedly." I knew she thought she was being helpful, but she really wasn't. "I'm fine, just cranky."

"Are you sure?"

"Yes." He turned his attention back to the road and I closed my eyes, trying to let the wave of nausea pass before I hurled all over Tate and his car.

"I know you don't believe me, Teddy, but I really am so damn sorry for running out the way I did. I shouldn't have, but my emotions were all over the place after dealing with those fucking cops." He smacked the steering wheel and I knew it was frustration at the memory — not me. "My head was all fucked up and you were part of that."

"Gee, thanks," I muttered but kept listening. Mildly intrigued.

"Sorry, but you were. In that police station, fierce as hell as you defended me. Got lawyers and told them what they needed to know to get me out of there. I appreciated that and it made me...hell, I don't know, crazy."

"I get it, Tate. You were tired of being my personal bodyguard. No harm in that. You have a right to your own life."

"Then you clearly don't fucking get it, Teddy. That night brought too much shit to the surface, shit I didn't want to deal with, like my time in prison, my anger." He let out a sigh. "And my feelings for you."

"And you realized you hated me and didn't give a damn if the stalker got to me?" I was trying for levity but I failed.

"That's not fucking funny," he said, as we pulled into the medical building parking lot. "I wasn't absolutely certain but I suspected it and it freaked me out, so I left. It was just supposed to be a ride to clear my head, but I rode and rode until my body ached. When I stopped I was just a few miles from Reno."

"That's a lot of riding and thinking." Apparently, he really did have a lot to think about.

He laughed but there was no amusement in it. "I did. I spent a couple days just walking around and trying to process everything. I should have called and made arrangements for your protection and I'm sorry for that, but I'm not sorry."

"Thanks, Tate," I snorted and slid from the car a second before I remembered I had a bum leg, a broken arm and a sprained wrist. "Shit!"

"I've got you, Teddy. Always."

I hated the way my body reacted at his closeness. But I missed him, dammit. At least my hormones had me convinced I did. "Thank you but I'm fine." I leaned against the car and waited for him to grab the wheelchair, and dropped into it with a loud sigh. "Let's get moving."

"We have ten minutes," he said gruffly, turning the chair around so we were face to face. "I'm not sorry because that time away gave me a chance to sort through my feelings. To realize that what I felt for you was more than I bargained for. Hell, I didn't even understand it. But I do now. Teddy, I'm in love with you."

I sucked in a breath at his words, unable to believe them. Unable to process them. "What do you mean you're in love with me? That's not possible!"

I didn't know much about love but I knew you didn't walk away. You didn't abandon the other person the moment things got hard. I knew all about that. It had happened to me plenty growing up. And if that was love, I wanted no part of it.

"It damn well is possible! It's true. I haven't given you a reason to believe me or to believe in me, but believe this...I love you and I'm going to find a way to earn your forgiveness for leaving you vulnerable."

I looked away. I didn't do vulnerable or weak. That was how you got hurt. But somehow, this man made me vulnerable. Made me open my heart to the possibility of more. To him. "I don't know, Tate. How can you be sure?"

"Because I nearly died when you were in that accident. Driving up and down the streets of Mayhem looking for your car in a goddamn ditch, it tore me up, Teddy. I cried. Fucking cried when the last time I shed a tear was when my mom died. That's when I knew without a doubt that I loved you. That you own my heart and soul. My body." His voice dropped an octave, so serious it scared me. "I am more than sure, Teddy and I'm not a patient man. You will be mine."

I shivered at his possessive tone. Men had always wanted to possess me, but not in this primal way shining in his eyes. "This is about the baby."

"It's not about the damn baby! I mean, I want the baby and I'll step up and be the best dad I can be even though I don't even know what a good father looks like. But this is about us. You and me. Tell me you love me or tell me to fuck off, Teddy. But tell me something."

I opened my mouth, not sure what would come out. Not sure what I even wanted to say but I couldn't say anything. My mouth was suddenly dry with black dots swimming around the edge of my vision. "I...uhm...Tate," and then everything went dark.

Chapter 23

Tate

Seeing Teddy faint, even from the safety of her wheelchair had shaved at least ten years off my life. One minute we were talking and I was holding my breath, waiting for her to let me down gently or declare her love for me, in her sassy, brash way, and the next I was carrying her in my arms through the ER doors, demanding they help her. To their credit, the nurses and the doctor moved as fast as any emergency room ever did, taking her vitals and pumping her full of fluids.

"Do you hear that?" The doctor wore a bright smile as a low *glug-glug* sound pulsed through the air.

I heard it and it sounded damn weird. It was fast and I knew it had something to do with the baby because of the big plastic wand rolling over her belly. "What is it?"

"It's the baby's heartbeat," Teddy said in a teary whisper.

"That's right, Mom. Your baby has a good, strong heartbeat."

Our baby's heartbeat. That left me stunned. I could hear my kid's little heart beating. "Is that too fast?"

"No, it's perfect," she assured both of us with a friendly smile.

I barely noticed her clean the gel off Teddy's belly, and the conversation between them came out muddled like I was under water. All of it suddenly became more real than it was even an hour ago. She was no more pregnant than she'd been then, but now the baby was real, even though Teddy was still as thin as she ever was. We drove home in a daze, after one of the most stressful three hours of my life, second only to the first twenty-four hours in prison. "Do you need any help?" I asked when I got her inside and back on the sofa.

Teddy rolled her eyes but I saw the small, sweet smile she tried to hide. "No, I'm fine. I'm going to try and clean the hospital stink off me." She looked away and sighed before turning back to me. "Thank you, Tate. For being there for me. We'll talk over dinner?" She moved to the wheelchair and looked up at me again. Waiting.

I gave a short nod and disappeared into the kitchen, making as much noise as possible so I wouldn't hear the spray of the shower and think about the water droplets drip over the swell of her breast, down her long legs. I tried to push those thoughts out of my mind by thinking about the fact that she still hadn't said anything about us. I poured out my fucking heart and told her I loved her, but she kept her thoughts and feelings to herself.

Patience wasn't my strong suit, but I was trying to be the man Teddy needed me to be. The man she deserved. That man would've understood her reluctance to talk until she knew the baby was safe.

Instead, I tried to push it while we waited and she'd shut down completely.

So now I was in the kitchen, making a healthy dinner for the mother of my child. The only woman to ever hold my heart. By the time Teddy made it back to the kitchen wearing a smile and a pretty little dress, the potatoes were boiling and the steaks sat in marinade, waiting for the broiler. "Hospital stink gone?"

She laughed and shrugged. "As much as I can get it done without a shower."

"Duh. That's right. You can't get that thing wet. I could help, you know, and for once I don't mean it in a dirty way." But I smiled and wiggled my brows anyway, because I was a man and this woman was mine. I'd never pass up a chance to get dirty with her.

"Careful, Golden Boy, I might take you up on that offer."

"Please do," I told her as I drained the potatoes and put the steaks in the oven before turning to her. "It would be my pleasure and punishment to help you get clean." She smiled up at me and I had to blink because I thought maybe I saw love there, but it was gone so quickly I couldn't be sure.

"It smells delicious in here."

"I figured after that scare in the parking lot we could both use a good meal."

"I appreciate it, but you didn't have to."

This was starting to piss me off. "Teddy we both know I don't do shit I don't want to do, so cut it out." I brought all the food to the table and we sat across from one another, eating in silence. "I didn't know what exactly was good for the baby, but I knew those stinky ass cheeses weren't good and neither was shrimp. Can't go wrong with steak."

She hummed her agreement.

"Need me to cut it for you?"

She waved me away and forked the steak whole, lifting it to her mouth with a satisfied smile on her face. When half her steak was eaten, she sat back and looked at me.

"I'm sorry about lying about the baby, but I needed to wrap my head around it first. I couldn't let anyone else's opinion influence me."

I sighed, trying really fucking hard not to be offended. "You thought I would tell you to get rid of it?" If so, she definitely didn't love me because she didn't fucking know me.

Her blue eyes went so wide they practically bugged out of her head. "No, I thought you would urge me to keep it and I wasn't sure if that was the right decision." She blew out a breath, like it was a relief to get it out there.

But I frowned. "Because of me?"

She laughed but the sound was hollow and bitter. "No, Tate. Because of *me*. I don't know jack shit about how a family is supposed to behave. I'm not sure I even know how to behave." She snorted another laugh. "Every mother figure I've ever had in my life let me down and I wasn't sure I was willing to risk bringing a child into that."

"And now?" I had to know.

"Now I'm sure I'll do better. I'll read every mommy book under the sun, do my best by hovering and helicoptering and whatever else comes along to make sure this kid is the smartest, funniest, best kid around."

She was definitely certain. It was evident in her tone, in that look of fierce determination and that sexy smile she wore. But I only nodded, waiting to see if I played any role in this future she laid out.

"Then there's us," she began, taking in a deep breath and letting it out slowly. "You were...unexpected. Together we were...two ships in the night, maybe."

"And now? What are we now?"

She smiled again and nodded. "We are...us."

"You're not anything bitch. Golden Boy is mine, damn you!"

We both turned, startled at Sheena's yelling. How in the hell did she get inside the house?

I barked out, "No I'm not, Sheena."

"You are, dammit!" She had a gun, a simple nine-millimeter clutched between her shaky hands, wild eyes darting between Teddy and me. The table set for two between us. "Did I interrupt another romantic dinner? Did I?"

Teddy shook her head, skin pale and lips drawn and nervous. "It wasn't romantic, just dinner."

"Shut up, bitch! This is all your fault, coming around and flaunting your long legs and fancy gear. I was a good little bitch for years, now it's my turn!" She was so angry, so filled with rage I had a bad feeling about how this would end.

I kept my voice even. As even as I could with a gun in my face. "I was never yours, Sheena."

"But you could have been, Golden Boy. Don't you see? We could have been fucking amazing together. I'm the kind of bitch that could have made you club president but you passed me over." She shook her head, smacking it with her palm. "I had it all planned out. I would show you a good time, fuck your brains out after being without a woman for so long. I would've let you do anything, Golden Boy. *Anything!*"

Teddy snorted out a laugh and my eyes went wide with shock. Was she crazy?

Sheena turned on her and my heart leaped into my throat when the gun stretched out, pointing to her face. "You have something to say, whore?"

Teddy just sneered. "You're so wrong about everything, do you even care about the truth?"

"Teddy," I began, hoping to warn her not to poke the crazy ass bear.

"No, Golden Boy, let her speak. Let the little slut tell us what's on her slutty little mind. Go ahead," she waved the gun in Teddy's direction. "Speak, bitch!"

I had to give Teddy credit; she looked way calmer than I felt even as she surreptitiously covered her belly as her gaze settled on Sheena. "You're the one who brought us together."

"Liar! Fucking liar!"

"It's true. We were just friends of circumstance before. His brother is marrying my best friend. But then some crazy psycho started stalking me and Tate offered his protection. Then we really started spending time together and well, you know the rest."

"His name is Golden Boy, you stupid bitch!"

Teddy shrugged like Sheena didn't have a gun aimed at her head. "Either way, this is on you *Sheena*. I should thank you."

Sheena raised the gun level with Teddy's forehead and grinned with crazy eyes. "For ending your misery tonight?"

"No." Teddy turned her gaze to me and smiled. "For pushing me into the arms of the love of my life."

Sheena let out a little shriek of pain. "Are you fucking serious right now? I have the gun so you both will fucking listen to me. To me!"

Teddy was like a freight train and wouldn't stop. I was sending her thought messages. *Baby, she's crazy, please, stop. She'll kill us.* But she just barreled on.

"You interrupted our evening, Sheena, not the other way around. This was a private conversation and since you're trying to steal my man, I figured it was the perfect time to step up."

Teddy looked back at me and grinned. "I know I have the worst timing in the world, but I figured this was a now or never type deal. I love you, Tate. I am madly, crazily, sappily in love with you. So much that I just want to hop on your lap and run my fingers through your hair like Jana does to Max."

I barked out a laugh over my pounding heart. We had to be delirious. It was the only explanation for both of us to be laughing and staring at each other with googly eyes as a crazy woman held us at gunpoint. "I like that," I said, my voice as shaky as Sheena's hand holding the Glock.

I don't know if Sheena was high or what but she quickly snapped, "Oh, please! Don't listen to her, Golden Boy, she's full of shit. A girl like her, she doesn't want a biker. She wants you for your money."

And then the lights went on. Thank you, Sheena. Suddenly it was all very clear. My breath started to calm and I took my eyes off Teddy and faced Sheena, shaking my head. What a dumb ass I'd been. If I hadn't had my head up my ass about being so pissed off about being falsely accused and the raw deal I got from the government and all that shit maybe I could have seen what was right in front of my eyes. But no. I had to put Teddy's life on the line *and* make everything about me. I went running off to Reno and all that shit and I still didn't figure it out. What the fuck took me so long?

"Goddammit, Sheena. Now it all makes fucking sense. You focused on me because *you* want the money." The next laugh came out harsher. Louder. "Of course you do. There are plenty of guys you could've tried to get it on with, and now I know why they wouldn't do. The money."

Sheena didn't blink an eye. "Okay, well, this has been fun and all, but I came here to get my man." She raised her arm again so the barrel of the gun was aimed right between Teddy's eyes. "And the only way to do that is to make sure you're not around anymore."

But Teddy didn't blink, either. "Do what you have to do, Sheena. Just remember that Tate won't visit you in prison. Will you, baby?"

I shook my head and thought this must be the most surreal night of my life.

"Never. Sorry," I told Sheena, because one of us had to try and keep the crazy bitch happy.

"That's okay, I have no plans to get caught. We'll use some of Golden Boy's money to get out of here, and by the time they find you we'll be on a beach somewhere sipping ice cold beers. You'll just be a memory."

The next few seconds happened in slow motion. Teddy's hands went to her belly and I knew it was coming but I couldn't stop it. "And he'll love being by the side of the woman who killed his first child. Won't you, babe?"

I knew it would either piss Sheena off or send her over the edge. She shot me a look that dared to cut me in half, then turned back to Teddy. "You're lying! You're a lying fucking bitch."

"Maybe I am, who knows? You'll only find out after the fact."

What was she doing? I put up my hand, as if that was going to stop Teddy. She had fire in her eyes. "No, babe. Do you want her to kill you?"

I knew she was a fighter, but it seemed like she was just giving up, asking Sheena to pull the trigger. I'd never felt so helpless in my life.

"I can't change her mind, Tate, and I refuse to feed her delusion." Those were the last words she spoke as the front and back door burst open at the same time and a dozen officers stormed the house.

"Down on the ground, right now! On the fucking ground!" I moved slowly, lifting my arms over my head and slid to the floor.

"On the fucking ground!" I couldn't see what was happening but I heard it all.

"I don't think so, pigs! If I can't have him ..."

Two shots sounded and a body collapsed to the floor. Teddy screamed.

"Fucking pigs, you shot me! I'll sue you all!"

"On the goddamn ground right now or I'll shoot you!"

"I can't, you asshole!" Teddy's words were distorted by tears and fear. But at least she wasn't dead.

"I'm in a wheelchair and I'm pregnant!"

"She's the vic," a deep voice I recognized as Detective Haynes said, seconds before he was lifting me off the ground. "You all right?"

My gaze went to Teddy. "I'm fine," I told him and dropped to my knees in front of her, wrapping my arms around her waist. "Are you okay?"

She nodded quickly. "A little sh-sh-shaken, but okay." Her smile wobbled, giving away her fear.

"You're okay, baby. I'm right here, the man you love."

She laughed. "You couldn't wait to rub it in, could you?"

"I just wanted to get it out there on the record." I turned to see the cops cuffing Sheena, a paramedic attending to her wound.

"With witnesses." Teddy laughed and it was the sweetest sound, light and airy, full of life.

With her uninjured hand, she cupped my jaw and leaned in for a kiss. "I love you Tate Ellison."

"Are you fucking crazy? You know she could have shot you."

"Baby, I looked at her and you and thought about baby Tate and decided I was done being afraid. She's been ruining my life these last few months and it pissed me off. It was time to take my life back. Maybe I'm pumped with too much adrenaline or baby hormones, I don't know. But something inside me said enough. I saw she had as much fear in her eyes as bravado and if she gave me the chance, I was going to knock the shit out of her with this cast or die trying. But she wasn't going to ruin my life anymore."

I put my arms around her and while Haynes and his team finished up their business, Teddy whispered in my ear, "She had also broken through the security code at the front door and knew the cops were on their way, so I might not be as brave as you think."

Chapter 24

Teddy

One month later

"Is this what normal is? It's been so long I forgot." Lounging in Jana's backyard felt so much like old times that my heart actually sighed.

"This is our new normal, I suppose," Jana said, beaming. "Old *about to be married* ladies with babies on the way." She glowed as she rubbed circles on her growing belly. At six months, she was all baby belly, smiling and damn near radioactive. "It's nice though, isn't it?"

Damn straight it was. "Yeah, I enjoy having no one try to kill me." Aside from a few extra trips to the doctor and talking to the cops, the past month had been pretty great. Things between Tate and I were better than ever. I was practically living at Max's old house because it would be a long time before I was able to stay at my place without nightmares.

After the blow up, Sheena had been handcuffed and shoved into the back of an ambulance, the whole time screaming for her precious Golden Boy to get her a lawyer so they could be together. It was sad and embarrassing, and if she hadn't tried to kill me and burn my house down, I might've had an ounce of sympathy for her. I didn't. "At least Sheena will be spending a long time in prison."

Jana looked over her shoulder with a worried look. "I think the guys are worried what she might try to offer up to reduce her sentence."

I blinked and tried to sit up, eager for the cast to come off in a few weeks. "What do you mean? I thought they were on the right side of legal?"

Jana sighed. "They're legal, but the gun thing is in a…grey area. And who knows what she might have overheard."

Well, shit. "I thought she made a deal already?"

"She did, but none of that matters until the papers are signed. The club paid for her lawyer so we'll have word soon enough."

I sat back and thought about what Jana said. Sheena could still pose a problem for Tate and all of the Reckless Bastards. "And you're sure they're not the kind of motorcycle club to knock people off?"

Jana laughed so loud she had to grip her belly, which sent Max running in our direction with a worried scowl on his face. "What's wrong, babe?"

She huffed out a breath between laughs, clutching her breath. "Oh good," *huff, huff,* "Teddy asked," *huff, huff,* "if you guys offed people." More fucking laughter.

Max frowned and then looked at me like I'd grown three more heads. And then he also burst out laughing.

"It's not like we haven't thought about it," Tate said as he dropped a kiss on top of my head. "But she knows we can make it very difficult for her on the inside."

I smiled up at him. "My little bad ass biker dude."

Tate leaned in with a panty-melting grin on his face. "We both know there's nothing little about me, sweetheart."

Amen to that. "I know. I can't wait to get some of that juicy, sizzling meat in my mouth." His gaze darkened intensely. "I'm starving."

"Very funny." He leaned over and brushed a gentle kiss behind my ear. "You're lucky I love you."

I was damn lucky and I knew it. It wasn't just having the love of a man as good as Tate, it was that feeling of being loved and being *in* love. The security and satisfaction of coming home to his smiling face and waking up in his strong arms. But it was worrying about him and hearing him talk about his day, the way his eyes lit up as he tried out things for GET INK'D. Just being together was pure bliss. "And you're lucky I love you too."

"I know it every damn day, Cover Girl."

I laughed. "Just for that, you're sleeping on the couch, Golden Boy."

"Yeah right, how will you sleep without rolling on top of me every night?"

He was right. Pregnant me preferred to use Tate as a body pillow and every morning I woke up completely wrapped around him, and he woke up soaked from the furnace hug. "I'll manage."

"Hey none of that right now," Jana insisted with a wag of her finger. "Save that for later, otherwise I'll never get to talk to Teddy about the wedding." She squealed excitedly. "I was thinking Hawaii, but maybe we should do a beach wedding in San Diego? What do you think, Teddy?"

Hawaii would likely be out of the question for Jana anyway with her pregnancy so far along, and maybe even for me as well. "I think it would be pretty hilarious to watch a bunch of bikers descend on the little tourist town."

"Oh, me too! But they have a really nice hotel there and we could hold everything there from the rehearsal dinner to the wedding reception."

"That's a great idea! Give me the dates and I'll get it all set up."

She squealed and tried three times to get up without success. "Damn constantly changing center of gravity."

Max helped her up and she came and hugged me tight, around both of our growing bellies. "You are the absolute best! And I promise when it's time for your wedding, I'll help too."

I laughed because we both knew that was a joke. Jana would have to be pulled, kicking and screaming, and that was fine by me. "Sure, you will."

She laughed and hugged me again. "Promise."

"Did someone say food?" Max and Tate stood above us, casting long shadows. But they held plates overflowing with succulent steaks and Jana and I both clapped with excitement.

"Yes, please!" I held my hands out greedily. "Food."

"You only want me for my food," Tate teased.

"And your body. Don't forget your totally hot body." He barked out a laugh and handed me the plate.

"I can't wait to make you mine," he growled in my ear, dropping something on my lap.

I looked down at the butter yellow sundress I wore and found a tiny turquoise box. "Tate," I said, a warning in my voice. "What is this?"

"That," he pointed with a satisfied grin, "is a promise. A proposal for forever."

"I'm listening."

His grin widened. "You know I'm not good with talking about my feelings and shit, but I love you with everything in me. You and our baby, and I want us to be a family. Theodora Elizabeth Quinton, will you be my wife?"

All the months of hell and uncertainty had brought us to this moment. Circumstances brought Tate and I together, attraction kept us together, but it was a deep and lasting love that would push us toward forever. So I looked at my golden-haired biker with love shining in my eyes and said the only thing I could. "Hell yeah, I will!"

And right there in Jana's backyard, surrounded by those who mattered, we got started on our little family and our huge forever.

~ THE END ~

Acknowledgements

Thank you! I love you all and thank you for making my books a success!! I appreciate each and every one of you.

Thanks to all of my beta readers, street teamers, ARC readers and Facebook fans. Y'all are THE BEST!

And a huge very special thanks to my wonderful assistants and PA. Without you, I'd be a *hot mess! I'm still a hot mess, but without your keen sense of organization and skills, I'd be a burny fiery inferno of hot mess!! Thank you!

And a very special thanks to my editors (who sometimes have to work all through the night! *See HOT MESS above!) Thank you for making my words make sense.

Copyright © 2018 BookBoyfriends Publishing LLC

About The Author

KB Winters is a Wall Street Journal and USA Today Bestselling Author of steamy hot books about Bikers, Billionaires, Bad Boys and Badass Military Men. Just the way you like them. She has an addiction to caffeine, tattoos and hard-bodied alpha males. The men in her books are very sexy, protective and sometimes bossy, her ladies are...well...bossier! Living in sunny Southern California, with her five kids and three fur babies, this embarrassingly hopeless romantic writes every chance she gets!

THEY CALL ME GOLDEN BOY.
AND I WENT TO PRISON FOR A CRIME I DIDN'T COMMIT.
OUT NOW, I'M A MILLION PLUS RICHER FOR THE SCREW UP,
WITH A SWEET TATTOO JOINT AND MY CLUB,
THE RECKLESS BASTARDS WATCHING MY BACK.
BUT WHEN TEDDY CALLS AND TELLS ME SHE WANTS INK
TO COVER UP HER PAIN,
MY WHOLE WORLD IS TURNED UPSIDE DOWN.
SHE'S TROUBLE WITH A CAPITAL T.
AND WAY TOO CLOSE TO HOME.
SHE'S TOO GOOD. ESPECIALLY FOR A DOG LIKE ME.
THEN I FIND OUT SHE HAS A STALKER.
I'LL F*CK UP ANYONE WHO TRIES TO HARM HER.
BECAUSE SHE MAY NOT KNOW IT YET,
BUT SHE'S ALL MINE.

KBWINTERS.COM